THE EXPEDITIONERS

THE
EXPEDIT

Harlow Brook Books

IONERS

and the
Lost City of Maps

by S. S. Taylor

Illustrations by Katherine Roy

This one is for my readers

THE
EXPEDITIONERS

SIMERIAN
MOUNTAINS

SNAKE
GATE

MAP OF
SIMER CITY

LEOPARD
GATE

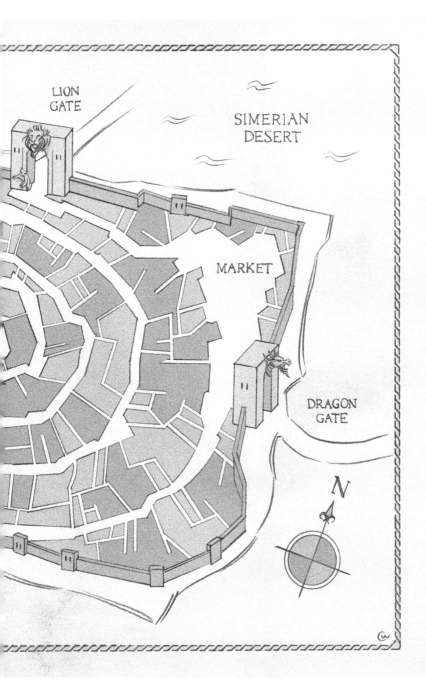

LION GATE

SIMERIAN DESERT

MARKET

DRAGON GATE

N

One

"We'll be arriving in Gryg City soon," a BNDL agent called through the half-open door of the baggage compartment. "Mr. Mountmorris says you can come up to the front if you want to see our arrival."

I made my way through the piles of suitcases and trunks, and along the narrow passageway that led to the main passenger areas of the big government airship.

The lounge in the central gondola was filled with people—black uniformed BNDL, or Bureau of Newly Discovered Lands—agents, government officials, and other trainee Explorers like myself from the Academy for the

Exploratory Sciences. We were all on our way to Grygia, and we crowded around the floor-to-ceiling windows of the gondola to watch the jagged peaks of the Carpathian Mountains rise up below us.

The airship was moving fast and for a terrible moment I thought we were going to hit the snow-capped mountains in front of us. But just when it looked like all hope was lost, we soared up and over them and then we were looking down at the wide white and dark green bowl of the Grygian Valley, the huge Grygian fir trees poking out of the heavy snow cover. It was early January, deep winter in Eastern Europe.

Grygia had been the first of the New Lands to be discovered, and its discovery had kicked off the New Modern Age of Exploration. Unlike us, Harrison Arnoz had made his way up and over these mountains in the early spring. He'd found a greener, more alive valley, filled with unknown species of ancient, towering trees, and the Grygian Tree Dwellers living in their intricately-constructed treehouses, complex networks of bridges connecting them to other trees and Tree Dweller communities.

But I knew that I was seeing what he had seen—from a different vantage point—and it was thrilling.

As we descended, the streets and buildings of Gryg City came into focus. The slopes of the mountains directly surrounding the city were covered with Grygian fir trees, but not far outside, huge swaths of the mountainside had been completely cleared. I could see big machines moving around in the logging camps. And at the other end of the valley, I could see the huge holes that had been dug into the hillside for the Gryluminum mines. The Gryluminum pits and strips of treeless ground looked like wounds and scars on the surface of the mountains.

"Hey! Baggage boy, you'd better get back to your work. We're almost there."

I looked up into the jeering face of my Academy classmate Lazlo Nackley, standing by the windows with his friend Jack Foster and another classmate, Kemal Asker.

"Come on, Lazlo, leave him alone," Kemal said, giving me an apologetic shrug. I liked Kemal and I knew he hated the way Lazlo had been treating me.

"What? It's true. Mr. Mountmorris is going to need his bags. And you're his baggage boy." Lazlo laughed.

My brother Zander and our friend Sukey Neville came running into the gondola, Zander's trained parrot Amerigo Vespucci on his shoulder. Sukey was wearing her uniform as a member of the trainee flying corps, an olive green flight suit, tall brown leather boots, and a brown jacket with a bright red "ADR Flying Squad Trainee" patch on it. Her copper-colored curls were pinned up on top of her head, but a few had escaped around her face. Sukey was a Neo, or Neotechnologist, but without her bright clothes made from synthetic materials, she looked just like all the other trainee pilots.

Except for the tiny green lights embedded in her ear. They blinked at me a few times before resuming a steady glow.

Zander was wearing his black ADR Officers Training Corps uniform, just like Jack and Lazlo. "Hey, Kit. They let us watch from the cockpit," Sukey said. "It's amazing. I thought we were going to hit the mountains, but we didn't. Oh, look! There's the aerodrome."

We were descending now, very slowly. Below, I could see the wide landing platform of an aerodrome. Smaller airships bobbed on their platforms. Suddenly, there was a loud rushing sound and a glider raced along the ground below us and rose up into the sky with a roar.

"It's a flying machine," someone shouted. "One of the new gasoline engine ones!"

We all watched as it flew up dangerously close to the gondola's window and then disappeared up into the sky.

"*Whoosshhhhh*," Pucci chortled, mimicking the sound of the flying machine.

"It must be a test flight from the ADR base outside Gryg City," Sukey said. The Agency for the Defense of the Realm was building military bases all up and down the border with the Indorustan Empire, and now that we were at war with the Indorustans they were moving soldiers and pilots to all of them.

I turned around and met Sukey's eyes. She was on her way to finish her training at the base. It would be her in the flying machine in a few weeks or months.

"Where's M.K.?" I asked them. My little sister had spent most of the voyage down in the control room. I missed her. Sukey shrugged. Zander said he hadn't seen her.

"See you later," I told them. "The baggage needs me."

I headed back to the baggage compartment. I had to repack Mr. Mountmorris's bags before we landed and then carry them off the airship myself. He didn't allow anyone else to touch them, which would have been flattering except that I hated him and I found it a little humiliating to have to organize his underwear.

Another black-suited, scowling BNDL agent was stationed outside the door to the baggage compartment and he eyed me up and down as I approached and said, "Mr. Mountmorris wants to see you. He's in his berth."

"But I thought I was supposed to get his bags together. We're about to dock."

"That was the order. You'd better hurry."

Mr. Mountmorris was in the fanciest of the passenger berths. I had spent the voyage sleeping in a cramped boxlike berth next to the baggage compartment, on the bottom bunk, beneath an engineer who snored and talked in his sleep about someone named Carla.

When I entered, Mr. Mountmorris's assistant, Jec Banton, nodded at me. Mr. Mountmorris was sitting at a table pulled up to the window so he could see the view. The table was laid with a teapot, cups, and a plate of cupcakes and pastries decorated with bright green frosting.

"Hello, Mr. West," he said, without turning around. "We are almost there. Exciting, isn't it? Your first trip to Gryg City."

His thin hand hovered over the cupcakes. Finally he chose one, plucking it off the plate as though it were a flower in a garden. I watched him lick the frosting from the top before putting it down.

"It would be if I knew what I was doing here." I paused. "Sir."

He turned quickly and fixed his eyes on me. He must have had lots of different pairs of colored lenses to go in his eyes. When I'd first met him, they'd been green. Today they were a deep shade of violet.

"You want to know what you're doing here, do you?"

"It would be really nice," I told him. "I've been in top secret clandestine services training for the past six months. I've learned how to survive in the desert, to trail someone for ten hours without being caught. I've learned how to make a weapon out of a dinner fork and to make basic conversation in thirteen languages. I know how to find a meal in the rainforest and I can find a perfect hiding spot within twenty seconds of walking into almost any room. And now, I am on my way to Grygia as your 'baggage assistant,' which seems to involve a lot of organizing of your socks. *Yes, I would like to know what I'm doing here.*" I'd been holding in my anger for a long time and it poured out of me now. It was hot in the berth and sweat trickled down my right temple.

Mr. Mountmorris smiled and waved a hand toward the window, and Gryg City beyond. "You are here to carry out a top secret mission in accordance with your training," he told me.

"Oh, right," I said sarcastically. "Yes, the top secret handling of the baggage. Will my mission involve socks or underwear today, Mr. Mountmorris?"

Jec Banton raised his eyebrows in disapproval, but Mr. Mountmorris just smiled and chose another cupcake.

"Mr. West, do you know how much your training over the last six months has cost the Bureau of Newly Discovered Lands? No? Well, let me tell you. More than one thousand Allied Dollars per day. As you say, you have had courses in world languages, in self-defense, in code-breaking and cartography. You know how to find water in a barren desert and you know how to disappear in any city in the world."

He waited a moment, then asked me, "Do you think that we would spend that much money on you if we meant to have you manage baggage for the entire trip?"

I gulped. "No, I guess not."

"Do you think that maybe, just maybe, we need to be careful about how we insert you into Simeria? Because there are many people who are interested in what our intentions are there and the moment you step off this airship you will surely be followed by clandestine agents of the Indorustan Empire?"

"I suppose that yes, that would make sense." I kept my eyes on the green cupcake in his hand.

"And do you think that perhaps this mission is all part of your cover? You do remember the lessons on creating a cover, an acceptable public identity that allows you to achieve your clandestine aim, do you not?"

"Oh, this is all my…? Oh," I gulped. "Sorry."

"Apology accepted. Now, Mr. West, I was just about to tell you that when we have arrived in Gryg City and I have had the afternoon to settle in at the Royal Grygian Hotel, I would like you to come and see me in my suite and I will brief you on your mission."

"O–o–okay," I stammered.

"And remember what I said about you being followed. For the moment, you must make no effort to go undetected. In fact, it would be good if you were seen walking around Gryg City. You are a trainee Explorer, coming along on my diplomatic mission as my baggage handler. You may act as though you are exactly that."

At that moment, the airship bumped gently against the landing platform. I heard a loud whoosh as the burners slowed. Through the windows, I could see workers scurrying around on the platform, securing the airship with ropes.

"Oh look," Mr. Mountmorris exclaimed cheerfully, his face now as bright and joyful as a kid's on Christmas morning. "We're here!"

Two

G ryg City was laid out in a grid at the base of the mountains that rose sharply above the city. Most of the buildings were made of huge, dark timbers, with steeply peaked roofs and carved wooden trim. Against the fir trees that covered the mountains near the city, they looked like something out of a fairy tale.

The main thoroughfare, Arnoz Avenue, spread out on both sides from the large three-story building that was BNDL's center of administration. Down the street was the towering Royal Grygian Hotel.

I was so loaded down with Mr. Mountmorris's luggage that I could barely see my surroundings, but Lazlo Nackley's constant narration gave me a sense of all the wonderful things I was missing.

"Look at the stones they used to build the hotel. Some of them are boulders. And look at the scenes painted on the roofline," Lazlo was saying. "Wow, it's beautiful here."

"It's been much too long since I stayed at the Royal Grygian," his father said. "I forgot how absolutely *heavenly* it is." Leo Nackley was one of the most famous Explorers in the world.

If Zander, Sukey, or M.K. had been there, I would have rolled my eyes at them. In addition to being a famous Explorer, Leo Nackley was a pompous jerk, a vain, mean, vindictive man who I was pretty sure would kill me for my father's maps if he got the chance.

I craned my neck, and in the tiny sliver of space above between Mr. Mountmorris's leather suitcase and his blue velvet hatbox, I could see painted scenes of Harrison Arnoz's arrival in Grygia running along the top of the hotel's facade. One panel showed him standing on top of a mountain peak and looking down at the Grygian Valley. Another showed him greeting the Grygian Tree Dwellers.

Someone pushed open a door and I was about to go

through it when it slammed back and hit me, knocking all the bags out of my arms. Kemal helped me pick them up, whispering, "Lazlo did that on purpose."

"Thanks, Kemal."

"He's being awful. I think he's just mad that you got invited along on what was supposed to be his special trip with Mr. Mountmorris." Kemal whispered.

"Come on, West," Leo Nackley said once we were inside. "Hurry up. Mr. Mountmorris wants to get settled in his room." From behind his father, Lazlo just smirked at me.

Zander, Sukey, M.K., Joyce Kimani and the rest of the trainee Explorers from the Academy were heading straight for the ADR base, but for some reason Lazlo and Kemal and I were getting special treatment and were staying at the hotel.

Well, they were getting special treatment. I was carrying one hundred pounds worth of Mr. Mountmorris's wardrobe.

The lobby of the Royal Grygian was paneled in dark wood, with luxurious couches all around, and bouquets filled with evergreen boughs and sprigs of red and purple berries. A big Christmas tree against one wall was decorated with delicate paper ornaments.

"Mr. West, please bring the bags along," Mr. Mountorris's assistant, Jec Banton told me. I gathered them up as best I could and followed his bright red, spiky Neo hairstyle up the wide, gold-painted staircase. He turned to wait for me but didn't offer to help, instead looking me up and down as though I were a plate of rotting fish.

Mr. Mountmorris's suite of rooms was at the back of the hotel, with a spectacular view of the mountains. The walls were covered with dark green wallpaper painted with scenes of men on horseback hunting the Grygian bear. I put the bags down on the gold-painted trunk at the foot of the huge bed and came out to find Mr. Mountmorris standing at the window, looking at the expanse of green and white. Jec Banton was organizing a stack of papers on the desk.

"It's quite something, isn't it? All this unspoiled wilderness?" Mr. Mountmorris asked me.

"Except for the fact that they're digging giant holes in the ground and cutting all the trees down."

Jec Banton looked up and I thought I detected the tiniest hint of a smile on his lips.

"Well, they're not cutting them down right there," Mr. Mountmorris said. "Jec, I'm thirsty." I heard a loud pop and Jec Banton came over with a glass of something that looked like champagne. "Ah," Mr. Mountmorris said, sipping from the delicate crystal glass. "That's better. Now, Mr. West, are you ready to hear your assignment?"

I didn't trust myself to say anything without revealing my frustration with the long months of waiting, so I just nodded.

Mr. Mountmorris stood up and went over to the desk. "Mr. Banton, will you please bring us the map?"

Jec Banton opened one of the bags and unrolled a large map, bringing it to Mr. Mountmorris and laying it out on the desk. The map showed Simeria—Simer City and the surrounding desert. The desert was a wide empty expanse of beige running right into the black line that was labeled "Indorustan Empire."

The desert itself was labeled "Unknown."

Mr. Mountmorris's finger hovered over the small bit of desert next to the black line. "The objective of your mission is to secure maps of the northern Simerian border with the Indorustan Empire."

I looked from Mr. Mountmorris to Jec Banton and then back again.

"But, I thought nobody has maps of that part of the desert. Every map I've ever seen looks just like that." I pointed to the word *Unknown*. "Nobody's ever been there."

"That," Jec Banton said. "Is not true."

"No," Mr. Mountmorris agreed. "It's not true at all. In fact, someone *lives* there. A man named Count Grigory von Rostovich. He has built a giant palace in the desert, very close to the Indorustan border. And we believe he has a map."

"But how do you know?"

"There are traders, nomadic people who live in the desert and who supply him with goods from Simer City. Our spies have heard rumors about Count von Rostovich for years, but no one has ever actually seen him."

I traced the empty desert with my finger. "So where do I come in? If you want to get his maps, why don't you just send the army over there and take over the palace or whatever?"

Mr. Mountmorris just stared at me. After a long moment of silence, he said, "Would you like to try again, Mr. West?"

"What? I…" I was flustered. It hadn't seemed like an unreasonable question.

"What?" he said in a high, whiny voice, making fun of me. "Would you like to *think*, Mr. West? Try to recall some of the geography lessons we took such great pains to deliver to you, and then try again?" His eyes narrowed in contempt.

My heart beating faster, I called up the map of Simeria in my head. *Geography. Geography. What did he mean?* In a training session just a few months ago, I'd learned that Simeria had remained hidden for so long because it was surrounded by desert. It still hadn't been fully explored. I remembered the trainers talking about intense sandstorms that forced travelers in the ancient world to skirt the Simerian desert to reach Greece and Europe.

"The sandstorms," I said. "Simer City is surrounded by desert and there are frequent and violent sandstorms. They're hard to predict. No one's been there because of the sandstorms."

"There you go," Mr. Mountmorris said, a little sarcastically. "The sandstorms. We had one operative try to make his way across the desert on horseback. We assume that a sandstorm came up and he became disoriented and wandered off course. His body and the horse's body were found months later. Another operative was never seen again after he was observed talking to some traders outside of Simer City." He raised his eyebrows. "The nomadic traders are fiercely protective of the route they use to cross the desert. We have tried to buy the information from them, but we've never been successful. They seem to be quite afraid of Count von Rostovich."

Mr. Mountmorris took a sheet of stiff paper from Jec Banton and held it out to me. "Count Grigory von Rostovich."

It was a photograph of a large man wearing a top hat and flowing white robes. The photograph seemed to have been taken on a terrace overlooking a body of water. The man was laughing and gesturing out towards the water.

"Count von Rostovich was born in Minsk, deep inside the Indorustan Empire, 48 years ago. We don't know much about his early years—we don't know much about anyone living inside the Indorustan Empire when it comes down to it—but we first became aware of him when he arrived in Simeria and began a lucrative career as a businessman, importer, and banker, among other things. He became very rich and then he disappeared. From time to time we have received intelligence reports that suggest he has built a huge palace in the desert, very close to the Indorustan border. He has a network of traders who bring him goods, and he has made a fortune selling products from the Allied world to the Indorustans." Mr. Mountmorris hesitated. "And vice versa."

"While his palace is technically on Allied territory, he is an Indorustan subject and obviously sympathetic to the cause. We suspect that he is helping them to prepare for a full-scale invasion of Simeria by allowing his palace to be used as a base for Indorustan military leaders. They already control parts of East Simeria. If they could come in from the North, they might have a chance of sweeping into Simer City and using it as a base from which to invade Europe.

"Count von Rostovichs's palace is well hidden in the desert. Because of the sandstorms, we can't get there with any of our vehicles—the sandstorms destroy any glider or airship or IronSteed we take in there. But the count—and his network of traders—seems to be able to travel freely through the desert. We think there must be a safe route and that he has maps of that route."

"So you want *me* to go there?"

"Yes. We have intelligence that the palace is well-guarded by his security force. A number of agents have attempted to infiltrate the area. They have all disappeared. A soldier, a delegation of government officials, even a grown man trying to pass himself off as a trader, would raise suspicion. But I believe you may have success where we have had only failure."

"But how will I…?"

"I suspect that you will find a method once you arrive in Simer City. You remember the part of your training where you learned about developing a plan of action on the spot? How good clandestine officers take immediate stock of available assets and opportunities? Well, that's what you're going to do."

"Okay. But, how am I going to get to Simeria? Are you going to take me? Wouldn't that defeat the purpose of me trying to keep a low profile?"

"Yes, it would, Mr. West. You are going to do what many explorers have done before you. You are going to make your way down through Eastern and Southern Europe and across to Simer City, where you will devise your cover. You must make certain that you are not identified by Indorustan agents as a BNDL operative. You must also make sure that you are not identified as a BNDL operative by regular BNDL agents or any Allied military. I will not be able to protect you if this happens. I cannot emphasize enough that this is a top secret mission."

I wondered if I looked as terrified as I felt. I must have because he met my eyes and said, "I will be sending other clandestine agents to shadow you and to provide aid on your expedition. These agents may be useful to you in creating your cover and making your way across the desert."

"Who is it? How will I know them?"

"Don't worry about that. Any agent will reveal him or herself to you in due course, by uttering a particular phrase."

Mr. Mountmorris's eyes sparkled as he paused for a long, dramatic moment.

"My sister's cat had six kittens last week."

I stared at him. "What? That's ridiculous."

"No it's not. It's perfect. If someone says that to you, you know we have sent them and they can be trusted.

"My sister's cat had six kittens last week," Mr. Mountmorris repeated in a solemn voice.

"My sister's cat had six kittens last week," I said. I couldn't help it. I laughed.

Mr. Mountmorris scowled at me. "Now, I want you to go and walk around the city this afternoon. Make sure you are seen and that anyone who wishes to follow you is able to do so. Tonight, you and all of your fellow trainees will be my guests at a celebration in the Grygian Tree Dwellers Village. I predict you will enjoy the experience—you'll really get a feeling for authentic Grygian

Tree Dweller culture. I am going to arrange a disturbance that will allow you to slip away, and then you're on your own. You will make your way to Simeria any way you can. After you're gone, I will put out a story that you displeased me on the mission and that I sent you home on a commercial airship. That ought to do it."

"Is that all clear?" Mr. Mountmorris asked.

There were so many things that were not clear to me that I didn't even know where to begin, so I just nodded.

"Have you got everything?" Mr. Mountmorris asked Jec Banton.

"Yes." He gave an impatient nod and picked up a small leather backpack that had been sitting on the floor.

Mr. Mountmorris took the pack from him and dumped it out onto the bed. I stared. The bed was covered with money, stacks of Allied dollars and a bag of gold coins. "This is ten thousand Allied dollars in cash and gold pieces for you, Mr. West. I will not be able to get more to you if you run out, so you will have to be frugal. Do you think you can do that?"

"Ten thousand?" I stared at him. "How could I ever spend that? I couldn't spend that in a million years."

"You will be surprised at how much it costs to get oneself from Grygia to Simeria," Mr. Mountmorris said.

"Without being identified. But I appreciate your thriftiness, Mr. West. Perhaps you will bring me back some money when you return with the maps of the northern border." He took a thin length of fabric with a buckle on it from Jec Banton and held it up. "Now, put the money in this and wrap it around your waist under your clothes It has a zippered pocket. I don't have to remind you that the cash isn't particularly safe there—a body search would reveal its location—but at least it's hidden for the moment." I folded the money into the belt.

As we left the room, Mr. Mountmorris handed me the photograph of Count von Rostovich, which I looked at for a couple of minutes before handing it back.

"Now go out and make sure any Indorustan spies lurking around get a good look at you," he said. "Good luck."

Our eyes met for a minute and I thought maybe he was actually worried about me, but then I realized he must be thinking of the other agents who had tried to cross the Simerian desert.

He was probably thinking the money was all for nothing.

He was probably thinking that he would never see me again.

Three

The temperature was hovering below freezing and I was glad I'd gone back to my room and changed into my thermal hat and jacket and gloves made of ultra-warm Yak fiber. I'd put most of the money in a hidden pocket inside the backpack, then thought better of it and spread it between a couple of different pockets in my Explorer's vest, the waist belt, the backpack, and the inside of my socks. My feet were freezing, so I stopped at a shoe shop and used some of the money to buy a pair of bear fur-lined boots like the ones the Grygians wore. I stood outside the store for a minute to give any spies who wanted to follow me a good view.

Then I set off to explore the city.

Walking as slowly as possible, I kept my mind occupied doing something I had found myself doing more and more over the past nine months: I visited Dad's map. Or rather, I visited the version of Dad's map that I had drawn after my return from King Triton's Lair.

I had seen the map—a beautiful mosaic created from rocks and shells—in King Triton's Lair, during our expedition to the Caribbean, and memorized it before it was destroyed. I knew Dad had led me to it and I knew that he wanted me to visit the place on the map.

What I didn't know was why.

When I got home from the Caribbean, I realized that the map in my head was a map of Simer City. I created a version on paper that took into account what I now knew about the region. It was tucked away carefully in the inside pocket of my Explorer's vest, but I'd looked at it so many times I had it committed to memory.

At first it had struck me as strange. After all, Simer City was no longer a hidden place, as King Triton's Lair had been. Why would Dad want me to go there? But the more I studied maps of the capital of Simeria, the more I began to suspect there was a hidden message in the map. At first the map in my head had seemed identical to the ones I'd found in books and the newspaper. But as I'd examined them, I'd had the feeling there were some small differences.

I wouldn't be able to figure out exactly what they were until I got to Simeria, but I had a feeling the solution to the mystery lay in those differences. It was why I had agreed to train as a spy for the government and to be sent to Simeria.

As I walked, I pretended I was walking the ancient streets of the city. Here was the Lion Gate, at the northern entrance to the city. That way would be the Leopard Gate, to the south. Here were the stairs to the Old Mosque. I walked the whole city in my mind, just to make sure the map was still there, and then I bought a cup of thick, hot chocolate and found a bench to sit on, slowly coming back to this frozen city from the hot desert one in my mind. I sat there long enough that anyone who had followed me would have a good chance of spotting me. Then I stood up and started walking up Arnoz Avenue.

Gryg City was eerily quiet. Only a few men and

women dressed in long fur coats and hats walked the streets, but there were BNDL agents on every corner. I passed the tallest building in the city center, the headquarters of Allied Gryluminum Inc., and counted ten armed agents guarding the entrance. I was betting there were more stationed on the roofs of the buildings.

I stopped twice. The first time, I touched the arm of a woman wearing a BNDL uniform and asked for directions to the Grygia History of Exploration Museum. While she explained the way, I glanced around. There were a few people on the street, but no one who raised my suspicions.

The second time, I pretended I had to re-lace my boot and kneeled down on the sidewalk to work on it, while carefully looking up and down the street. This time, I noticed a thin man or boy dressed in a bright blue coat that reached down to the tops of his boots. He must have been a Neo because the coat was made of a shimmery fabric that looked synthetic and he was wearing a bright blue balaclava in the same fabric, which obscured most of his face. I stood up slowly and kept walking toward the history museum.

Once I was inside, I ducked behind a carved wooden post and watched the entrance. I waited a full ten minutes, but Blue Mask didn't appear. Either I had been wrong about him or he'd decided not to follow me. I relaxed and went to look at the exhibits.

The big main room was filled with exhibits about the New Golden Age of Exploration, the life of Harrison Arnoz, and the hidden or unexplored cities of the world. I spent a lot of time reading about the legends of cities in the ancient world, Palmyra and Babylon. Simeria itself, I was interested to learn, had been long-rumored but remained hidden because of the sandstorms.

The next room was filled with huge, life-size dioramas showing scenes of Grygia's history from its discovery by Harrison Arnoz to the present. The first one showed Arnoz greeting the Grygian Tree Dwellers. Another showed a group of Tree Dwellers smiling as a couple of men wearing BNDL uniforms used a saw to cut down a huge Grygian Giant fir tree. Another one showed a man holding up a piece of metal armor in front of the first of the Gryluminum mines. Again, there was a smiling group of Tree Dwellers looking on.

Suddenly, a man dressed in a long fur jacket and a fur hat was standing next to me and viewing the diorama. I started; I hadn't seen or heard him come up next to me.

"Ha," he said, in a voice I'd come to know very well.

"I don't think that's exactly how it was, do you?"

I caught myself before turning to look at him.

It was the Explorer with the Clockwork Hand or, as I now knew him, Marek.

"They haven't been teaching you much in spy school," he whispered. "If anyone's tailing you, you've given them about a hundred opportunities to lock on." Out of the corner of my eye, I saw him move his head just a tiny bit and his eyes crinkled at the edges in humor. "But maybe that was the point."

"I'm pretty sure someone followed me," I whispered, pretending to look at the painting. "He's not here. I'm not sure who it is, but Mr. Mountmorris thought that Indorustan agents might be interested in what I'm up to."

"I'm sure they are. What's going on?"

"I leave for Simeria soon, probably tonight. My mission takes me across the Simerian desert, but hopefully I'll be able to spend some time in Simer City first to figure out the map."

"You still have it?" He tapped his forehead.

"Yes, I still have it." Casually, I walked over to the next diorama, this one showing a family of Grygian Tree Dwellers in one of their traditional tree houses. Marek waited a few moments and then followed. There was a couple looking at the dioramas on the other side of the room, but they didn't seem very interested in us.

"Good. You must figure out why he left it for you and then you have to carry out your mission so no one will suspect the real reason you wanted to go to Simeria."

"So Mr. Mountmorris won't suspect, you mean."

"Of course. I'll be in Simeria as soon as I can, maybe even before you. I'll do what I can, but the city is crawling with spies. You'll have to be very careful, you know. It's a dangerous place. Even more so now we're at war. The East Simerians attacked the BNDL administration building last week. You're going to have to watch yourself."

"I know," I said quietly.

He reached inside his fur jacket and took out a book, which he handed to me. The cover read, *The History of Simeria*. "A little light reading for your trip." I tucked it into an inside pocket of my vest.

We both looked at the diorama. The scene showed a man and woman sitting together in a Tree Dweller treehouse.

"The Tree Dwellers love the trees they live in like members of their family," Marek said. "Many generations are born and grow up in the same tree. They say that the trees speak, that they sing babies to sleep at night. I once heard a man describe how the sound of a tree being cut down was like the scream of a man being murdered." He touched the glass. "What are you doing tonight?"

"Some sort of gala dinner in the Tree Dweller Village."

"Ah, yes. Local color."

"There's going to be some sort of disturbance and that's when I'm supposed to take off."

He looked concerned before saying, "Be careful. And goodbye." He strolled over to look at another diorama and then walked slowly out of the room and towards the main entrance.

I waited a few minutes before following him.

It was even colder outside now and a fine snow had started falling. I headed for the hotel, but not before noticing Blue Mask walking along the sidewalk on the other side of the street. It was too much of a coincidence. He had to be following me.

I walked slowly so it would be easy for him to tail me all the way to the hotel.

"Enjoy it while you can," I muttered under my breath. "After tomorrow, it won't be so easy to find me."

I was passing Mr. Mountmorris's door on my way back to my own hotel room when I heard Leo Nackley's voice coming through the paneled wood and slowed to listen.

He was angry about something. I'd been on the receiving end of Leo Nackley's anger enough times to recognize the tone. There was no one in the hallway, so I stopped and listened, my room key out so I could pretend to be opening my door if someone appeared.

"He's hiding something. I know he is!" Leo Nackley shouted. "I don't understand why you don't just arrest him and make him turn over the maps or whatever it is Alex gave him. I can only imagine what else they might lead us to."

Mr. Mountmorris's voice wasn't quite as loud but I could still make it out from the hallway. "Calm down, Leo. You know he won't have it on him. I'm handling that situation. You don't need to be so worried about it."

"Worried? I'm not worried. I'm just wondering why you're allowing a . . . a *child* who we suspect to be working against the interests of the country to come along on an important military mission as your assistant."

"Leo, Leo. Calm down. Don't you think that it's best to keep Mr. West close so we know what he's doing? I have a plan for him, and the plan requires me keeping track of him. I have lots of people watching. You have nothing to worry about."

A maid came down the hallway towards me so I kept walking to my door and opened it, smiling at her before going in. She might be one of the people Mr. Mountmorris had hired to watch me. Anyone might.

I stood for a moment in my empty room. For almost a year, I'd been training for hours a day by myself. I'd gotten used to being alone. But it was the first time it really struck me that I couldn't count on anyone but myself. It was a very lonely feeling and I shivered despite my warm jacket and boots.

high-tech plastic flight goggles

turquoise leather flight cap

lights embedded in ear lobes

copper colored curls

freckles

oar

amber eyes

synthetic flight jacket

pockets

glider tattoo

royal blue jump suit

cargo pockets

tall synthetic flight boots

SUKEY

Four

The line of SteamCars snaked along the narrow road to the Grygian Tree Dweller Village. The settlement, which had been built as a reservation for the Tree Dwellers after they were moved out of their treehouses, was about twenty miles outside of Gryg City and it took us almost an hour on the snow-covered roads, though it felt like three since I was riding in a car with the Nackleys.

"This is the first settlement built for the Tree Dwellers," the BNDL agent narrated as we chugged along. "It was built as a safe and civilized place for the Tree Dwellers to live once it was determined they could no longer live in the treehouses."

"Why couldn't they?" I asked.

"Because only animals live in trees, West," Lazlo Nackley sneered.

"We certainly think it's better for the Tree Dwellers to be housed in uh, healthy and sanitary buildings like those," the agent said, pointing to the six-story concrete block apartment buildings where the Tree Dwellers had been moved.

"But hadn't they been living in the trees for centuries and centuries?" I asked.

The agent ignored me.

"Why are you always trying to create trouble, West?" Lazlo Nackley said.

His father laughed.

I didn't say a word. I was thinking about tonight, wondering about the disturbance that Mr. Mountmorris had planned. I had more important things to worry about than Lazlo Nackley. But when I looked up, Leo Nackley was watching me, as though he was wondering why I hadn't responded to Lazlo's question. I thought about what he'd said to Mr. Mountmorris. He didn't know I was working for the government but he knew I was hiding something.

The SteamCar pulled up in front of a complex of buildings and a big sign reading, "Authentic Grygian Tree Dweller Village. The Ultimate Tourist Experience."

"Ah, here we are," the agent said. "I think you will enjoy your visit to a real, authentic, Tree Dweller Village. Now, mind your heads exiting the vehicle and follow the signs to the ladders. Here we go."

We followed a path through the trees lined with flaming torches. Agents stationed along the sides of the path guided us towards a set of wide wooden ladders. We climbed and came out onto a wooden platform high in the trees that was connected to other platforms by a series of bridges.

All around us were more of the bridges, linking all of the trees together, and in each tree there was a wooden structure, some of them quite large, with wide windows made of stretched animal skin or paper.

"This way, if you please." A man dressed in a heavy bearskin coat, his beard long and scraggly, his eyes wary underneath a bearskin helmet, pointed to one of the bridges radiating out from the main platform. We followed rows of torches along the bridge until we reached another huge platform, this one built up against what must have been twenty or thirty enormous

Grygian Giant fir trees. Tables and chairs were set up around a stage in the center. The air was filled with the smell of roasting meat and the sharp scent of the fir trees.

"You'll see here the famous Grygian Bear," called out a man dressed in a leather coat and high fur-lined boots like mine. I went over to investigate and found him standing in front of a wooden cage. Inside was a sad-looking Grygian bear, his giant body slumped in the corner of the cage.

I had seen many pictures of the bears with their huge, blocky heads and squared-off ears and other features that had told Harrison Arnoz he'd found a new species. But this was the first time I'd seen a real one. Instead of awe, though, I just felt pity.

"I'd like to let that bear out of that cage and see what it would do to him," Zander said behind me. Pucci whistled from his shoulder.

"I can arrange for the lock on the cage to break, you know," M.K. said.

"No." Zander ruffled her hair. "The poor bear probably wouldn't know what to do if he were set free."

"Hi, Kit," Sukey said, giving me a quick hug. Her cheeks were very pink from the cold and she had on a heavy brown parka made of a shimmery Neo material that made me think of the Neo who'd followed me today.

"Where'd you get that jacket?" I asked her.

"A shop out by the base. The flight suits aren't warm enough for this weather. Why? Are you okay? Where have you been?"

"I'm fine. I'm in a swanky hotel," I said. "Hot water and everything."

"Lucky," M.K. grumbled. "You should see the barracks where they put us. If I don't turn into a block of ice by the end of my training, it'll be a miracle."

"Well, at least the war's in the desert," Zander said. "We may get killed, but there'll be sun."

The Grygian bear roared and his trainer held up a hand and said, "Behold the Grygian Bear." He unlatched the door and the bear came ambling out.

"I don't like this," Zander whispered.

"Behold the killing machine of the Carpathians," the man shouted as more people gathered around to see what was going on. He held up a piece of meat and the bear began to dance in a slow, stilted way. Everyone except for us laughed and clapped. The man raised a hand in the air as though he were going to strike the bear and the bear cowered, causing the crowd to jeer again. I wanted to reach out and strike the man across the face.

"I can't stand it," Zander said. "Let's sit down."

We were shown to a table of dignitaries and other students from the Academy, including Joyce and Kemal.

"Feels like old times, doesn't it?" Joyce asked.

"I hope the food's better than the food at the Academy," M.K. said.

"Maybe Lazlo will join us and say something mean," Zander said. "Then it will really feel like old times."

"Uh oh," M.K. said. "You shouldn't have said that."

"I hope you're not going to complain about the food, West," Lazlo Nackley said, looking down at us. His father was behind him, talking to the BNDL employees at our table. They joined our table as Mr. Mountmorris jumped up to the front of the stage, next to the bear's cage. The bear was now locked up again, slumped miserably in a corner again.

"Please sit, please sit," Mr. Mountmorris called to us. "You are all my guests and I have a special treat tonight, some authentic Grygian Tree Dweller entertainment. Please relax and enjoy the ambience."

Three Grygian Tree Dwellers came out, carrying small guitars made of polished wood. They started playing and a few of Mr. Mountmorris's guests got up and danced a set dance, linking arms and swinging their partners around, and then switching partners and dancing to the jaunty beat of the guitars.

More Tree Dwellers came out with platters of food, mostly roasted meat with a few wrinkled carrots and parsnips thrown in. The meat smelled delicious.

"What is this?" I asked a woman sitting across from me. She was part of Mr. Mountmorris's delegation.

"Pepper Venison. It's a local specialty."

It was very good, spicy and rich-tasting, and M.K. and I had seconds from the large platter in the middle of the table. I reminded myself that I didn't know when my next real meal would be and I had thirds.

BNDL agents guarded the tables and I watched as one of the Tree Dwellers tried to leave the area but was stopped by an agent on the bridge. He argued with him for a few seconds and then the agent said something that made him stop and go back to stand with the other Tree Dwellers who were waiting on tables.

When we'd finished eating, the waiters served almond cake with berries on top, and pretty soon everyone was up and dancing. M.K. and Zander were acting silly, whirling each other around, and Joyce and Kemal joined them, jumping around and swinging each other by their elbows. Jack was dancing with a girl I recognized from the Academy and even Lazlo was moving stiffly from side to side in time to the music.

"You okay?" Sukey asked me.

I didn't know what to say. I wasn't okay. I was terrified. But my mission was top secret and I couldn't tell her anything about it.

"Me? Yeah, of course I am."

"You're going to Simeria, aren't you?" she asked me. I stared at her. Her eyes reflected the light from the torches behind me.

"Why do you say that?"

She winked. "Come on, Kit. I know about the map. And I know that you got recruited to be a spy. And I know that Simeria is where all the spies want to be. There's a war on. I, of all people, should know that."

"I can't say a word," I told her.

"Be careful," she said.

I looked at her for a long moment. "You too. And, Sukey. If something happens tonight, well, don't believe what they tell you. Okay?"

She nodded. "As if I would ever believe anything they tell me."

I looked into her eyes. "I shouldn't be telling you this, but if you need anything, if anything happens, write me a letter care of the post office in Simer City. Address it to, uh…" I thought, trying to make up a name.

"How about… Yoren Balloty?" she said.

"Yoren Balloty?"

"Yeah. I just made it up."

"Okay, though he sounds like a… shoe salesman."

She grinned and took my hand. "Do you want to dance?"

"I don't really… I'm not a…"

"Oh come on." She jumped up and pulled me to my feet.

The music was fast and jaunty. Sukey linked elbows with me and swung me around. I had to run to catch up, but it was easy to get the hang of the dance and allow ourselves to be carried along by the crowd of dancers. Zander was dancing at the other end of the crowd, swinging M.K. around and then weaving in and out of a group of dancers that included Joyce, Lazlo, Jack, and Kemal.

Sukey's copper eyes were bright in the torchlight. We spun and twirled.

I felt suddenly happy, as though the fires burning

along the edges of the platform were burning inside me, warming me, lifting me up. I grasped Sukey's hand and we spun again. M.K. flew by me and I wanted to reach out and hug her, tell her I might be leaving soon, but I knew it would seem suspicious. Sukey would just have to tell her.

I started to lean over to ask her to talk to M.K. but Zander took her arm and spun her away from me. She disappeared into the crowd of people.

The music stopped. Everyone moved to the edges of the platform and Mr. Mountmorris stepped out into the center of the circle again.

"We have a special treat for you tonight," he called out. "An exhibition of Grygian Tree Dweller sword dancing!"

I remembered hearing about the sword dancing rituals in a class at the Academy. They were part of traditional feasts, where the dances were performed to celebrate their winter holiday. The dances told the story of the Tree Dwellers' history and culture.

The musicians started playing at a faster tempo and a tall man with a long black beard, dressed in bearskin leggings and a fur cape came marching out onto the dance floor, holding a huge Grygian longsword. He started bending his knees in time with the music, still holding the sword out in front of him. Then a second man appeared, and a few minutes later, a third. They formed a circle and spun around, each of them holding out the sword and turning right and left. The music got faster as it went on and after about five minutes, three women arrived to dance with the men. They formed an inside circle and spun at a slightly faster rate than the men, so that a different woman ended up dancing with each of the men.

The women clapped their hands above their heads and turned in time to the music.

Suddenly, one of the men bellowed out loud and raised his sword above his head. The other men bellowed back and raised their swords too.

They faced off and began dancing towards each other, kicking their legs out to the sides and whirling around in formation.

A couple of BNDL delegates sitting at Mr. Mountmorris's table had had too much of the Grygian honey wine and they got up and pretended to dance, each holding a knife over his head and laughing as they mocked the Tree Dwellers.

The dancers kept dancing. There was something mesmerizing about the stamping of their feet and the wide arcs the swords made above their heads.

The music got faster and faster and the men stared at each other as the women continued to spin. Then one of the men shouted something, a loud exclamation that sounded like a battle cry, and the other man repeated the cry.

The men's bodies were absolutely still.

Suddenly, they had their swords in hand and were really fighting, the swords swinging over their heads and clanging together.

"Are they actually fighting?" a woman next to me asked.

"No," someone said. "It must be part of the performance." But the words weren't even out of his mouth when the agents jumped in and started punching one of the men. A gasp went up amongst the crowd and the agents moved in to protect Mr. Mountmorris and the other dignitaries.

People were jumping up from their tables to avoid the fracas. In the tight quarters of the treehouses, panic set in and people screamed and shoved each other to get on to the narrow bridges. Someone knocked over a torch and it ignited a pile of tree branches lying on the platform.

I stood there, paralyzed for a moment, before realizing that this was it. Somehow Mr. Mountmorris had arranged this. This was the disturbance that would allow me to get away. Sure enough, all the agents were focused on the fight and I slipped behind a tree and watched to make sure I hadn't been followed.

Then I ran along the nearest tree bridge, racing past a series of small, preserved tree house dwellings that were part of the Grygian Tree Dweller Village exhibit. Once I was a hundred yards from the fight, I ducked into an empty tree house, pressing myself against the inside wall and waiting again to see if I'd been followed. I remembered what I'd learned from my evasion training. You couldn't just test for a tail once. You had to keep checking.

No one came.

I set off across the bridge leading away from the entrance to the village. I'd be better off getting as far away from the fight as I could and then doubling back. I needed to completely disappear now, while people might be looking for me.

Because I was checking behind me, I didn't see the figure standing at the end of the bridge, leaning against the tree and blocking my path.

It was Leo Nackley.

And he was waiting for me.

Five

I considered my options.

If I doubled back, I'd run the risk of running into anyone else who'd followed me. And I didn't want to head back towards the entrance to the village, where the BNDL agents would be. I needed to keep going.

But Leo Nackley was in my way

"Where are you going?" he asked me coldly.

I didn't say anything. I needed to get past him, but he was a tall man who must have weighed twice what I did and and I was pretty sure he had had the same hand-to-hand combat training that I'd just completed. This wasn't a fight I wanted to have.

"I know your secret," he said, walking towards me. He was wearing a fur overcoat and hat, and he looked like a huge animal, the bulk of his chest and shoulders silhouetted in the faint moonlight showing through the trees. "I know that your father left you maps. I know that they lead to something important, something he thought it was worth risking his life for. I know you have them and I'm going to get them."

"Mr. Nackley," I said quietly. "I don't know what it is that you think I have, but you've got it wrong."

"I was his friend," he said. "I was on expeditions with him. I know he had a secret. Mountmorris says he doesn't know what it is, but he knows more than anyone thinks he does. Just hand it over, Kit."

"I wish I could, Mr. Nackley. If I had something to give you, I would. But I don't."

A bird called in the trees above us and he glanced towards the sound.

I knew this was my chance.

My left foot planted on the boardwalk, I took a deep breath and took off, sprinting past him towards other end of the boardwalk and the trees beyond. I had almost gotten to the other side of him when he reached out and managed to grab my leg. I crashed to the boardwalk and he was on top of me, holding my arms down, his face angry in the tiny bit of moonlight filtering through the trees.

"You are coming back to the village with me right now," he whispered. "And I am going to turn you over to Mr. Mountmorris's guys. They'll be able to get it out of you."

I waited a second, assessing my advantages and disadvantages. He was bigger and stronger, but I had access to his eyes and mouth now. One of the most important principles of the hand-to-hand combat methods I'd learned in training was that you needed to get yourself into a position to exploit the weaknesses of the human body—soft tissue and the parts of the face with many nerve endings.

"Okay," I said. "You win. I'll give you the map."

He sat up a little and I used that moment to drive my thumbs into his eyes and then roll out from under him. He was screaming and clutching his face, and I kicked him once in the stomach for good measure and then took off running down the boardwalk. I took a couple of turns to confuse him in case he managed to get up and follow me.

Soon, I was out of the restored part of the Tree Dwellers village, running along rickety bridges that had fallen into disrepair. I needed to get down and out of the trees. Leo Nackley knew I was up here and if he alerted BNDL agents, it was only a matter of time before they found me. Mr. Mountmorris had made it clear I was on my own. If they caught me he'd probably be able to stop me from being thrown in jail, but I would have ruined my chances of getting to Simeria. And I had to get to Simeria.

I ducked into another treehouse to see if he'd followed me.

I thought I was safe, but just as I was about to start running again, someone ran past my hiding place. It wasn't Leo Nackley, and whoever it was stopped right in front of the treehouse. In the moonlight filtering through the trees, I saw the shimmering blue balaclava covering most of my pursuer's face. It was the mysterious masked man from Gryg City. He looked back and forth as though trying to figure out where I'd gone, and then took off down one of the bridgeways. I waited and then started running in the opposite direction, toward the treehouses to the east.

It was a regular convention up here in the trees.

"Anybody else following me tonight?" I muttered to myself.

I needed to get down and out of the treetops and then I could make my way toward the mountains. My best bet was to get as far away from the village as I could, and then somehow try to get aboard a train leaving Grygia, but I was going to have to be creative.

In the distance I could hear voices coming nearer. Agents probably. I had to go. I leapt up and ran along the bridge through the old, original part of the Tree Dwellers village. When I reached a central platform with five bridges radiating from it, I stopped, unsure which way to go.

"This way," a voice said and I looked up to find a Grygian Tree Dweller, wearing a bearskin mask and fur cape and coming out of the thick overhanging branches. I got ready to defend myself if I had to, but he stood back and waved at one of the bridges.

"Go," he said. "Run. Take that one."

I had no idea who he was or whether he worked for the government, but I didn't have a lot of options and he seemed to know his way around the trees, so I followed him along the bridge. Behind me, I could hear pounding footsteps, but I didn't stop to see who it was. When I reached the end of the bridge, I jumped down into one of the trees and climbed down backwards to the ground.

When I was sure no one had followed me, I stopped to put on my hat and gloves and took off into the dark forest through the deep snow, my hands out in front of me, feeling for obstacles. I kept running until I had to stop to catch my breath. The forest was silent, the air thick with the scent of pine and the sharp, icy smell of snow.

"We are safe now," said a voice from the trees.

"Thank you," I panted. I was wary, ready to get my knife out of my vest or to run, but for the moment I needed to rest.

"That is okay." He stepped into the little bit of moonlight filtering through the trees and pulled off his bearskin mask. He was about my age, a tall, broad-shouldered boy who looked even bigger because he was covered in the heavy bearskins. "I'm Tarku."

I stared at him. "Kit. Why did you help me?"

"I saw you running away from the government party. I think you are trying to escape. Then I see that man chase you and I decide to help you. If you run from the government, then you are like me and I will help you."

"Well, thank you." I felt a little bit guilty. After all, *I* was a spy for the government. But he didn't need to know that.

He grinned. "It was nothing. Come on, follow me."

Tarku turned around and watched me try to run in the crusty snow and then reached up to pull down a couple of boughs from one of the giant fir trees. He took a knife out of a little holster on his boot and trimmed them, then used the long laces on my boots to lash the boughs to the bottom of my feet. With my improvised snowshoes, I was able to keep up with him and we covered a lot more ground. Moonlight made the snow-cloaked trees looked like shadowy figures in white clothes.

My heart was pounding with the effort, but after an hour or so of hiking, I started to notice a difference in the forest. It was hard to tell exactly what it was at first, but then I got it. The trees must have been groomed long ago. The huge trunks were completely bare and there was a thick canopy of growth up above.

They looked more like the trees in the Tree Dwellers Village.

"Up here," Tarku said. He grabbed on to something on the tree trunk and quickly climbed up and out of sight. I removed my makeshift snowshoes and examined the tree. There were a couple of places where a few short limbs had been left to provide footholds and handholds. It was easy to shimmy up after him and onto a dilapidated Tree Dweller village platform. To my right was an old bridge and I followed him past a couple of tree-houses that were falling in until he found one that was still mostly intact.

The walls of the treehouse provided some protection from the wind and chill outside. I turned on the light on my vest and looked around the single large room, with a shallow pit built into the center and lined with stones. Above was what must once have been a sort of chimney, but was now just a ragged hole in the ceiling. Still, it would offer an exit for smoke if we could manage to build a fire.

He watched me for a minute. "You have food?"

I thought about how to answer. I didn't have much and if I went through it too quickly, I was going to run out before I even got to Simeria. But he may have saved my life and it seemed wrong not to share.

"I have some dehydrated rations," I told him, taking them out and showing him what I had. "You're welcome to share."

He opened one of the packages and looked at it, then wrinkled his nose and said, "Good thing I took food from dinner." He removed a leather pouch from his jacket and opened it up. Inside was a big chunk of the venison we'd had for dinner, still warm, along with some vegetables and cake wrapped in paper.

"Is that why you were at the dinner?"

He grinned. "Yes. When they have a fancy dinner, it is easy to steal food if you know the bridges." I took a small piece of venison from him. I wasn't really hungry since I'd just eaten, but I knew it might be some time before I ate again.

"Do you live in the Tree Dweller village?" I asked him.

He looked at me incredulously. "No. I live out here."

"But I thought all of the Tree Dwellers had moved to the village."

"Moved?" He laughed. "No one moved. We were forced. The village is a prison."

"Okay, but why didn't they make you go there?"

He grinned at me. "You think they got everyone? Some people knew that they were coming. They went far up into the mountains and they stayed there. There are villages up there that BNDL doesn't know. Many, many people. Some were taken. My family was taken. We lived in the village. Went to school. Learned English. Many people got very sick from disease, so my father helped my brother and me escape when we were forced to work at lumber camp. He made an accident with a big machine and we ran away. So now I move from place to place so they do not find me."

"Where's your brother?" I asked him.

He looked very sad all of a sudden. "I do not know. He go out for firewood one day and don't come back. Maybe he get caught by government. Or bear."

"I'm sorry," I said.

He shrugged. "Why do you run from government?"

Of course I couldn't tell him, so I just said. "It's a long story, but I can't let them find me. I need to get out of Grygia. I have to figure out how to get out of here."

"Not train," he said. "They check train carefully."

"Could I walk?"

"Walk where?"

"Over the mountains?"

He laughed. "It is beginning of winter. It take you months and months. Maybe you die."

"Is there any way out?"

"I don't know. I will think about it."

Tarku sucked every bit of meat off the bones of the venison leg and tossed them over the edge of the platform.

"Bears will eat it," he said.

"Have you ever been attacked by a Grygian bear?"

"Once. I climbed a tree."

"Can't they climb too?"

"Not as fast as me." He grinned at me again.

We were quiet, listening to the wind. I hunched down into my jacket and pulled my hat down over my ears.

"It's really peaceful out here," I said. "Someone told me that the Tree Dwellers believe that trees can sing. I thought he was just making it up, but now I think I know what he meant."

"They say trees are alive, that they talk to us," Tarku said. "When I was very small and we live in the village, my mother tell me about how Tree Dweller babies were rocked to sleep by the trees, how the trees sing to you at night. Now I live in the trees, I think she right."

I was tired. I unfolded my reflective sleeping bag from its pouch in my backpack and got inside. Tarku wrapped his bearskins securely around his shoulders and lay down on the ground. The wooden floor was hard, but I didn't care.

The wind moved through the huge fir trees and the treehouse swayed gently, rocking us to sleep. I thought maybe I could hear the trees singing to us, an old song, but maybe it was just the creaking and groaning of the wood.

Six

I was awakened early the next morning by a series of loud, echoing booms across the valley and I jumped up, ready to run. When I looked through a window in the treehouse, I could see a layer of fresh snow on everything. I rolled up my sleeping bag. I had to be ready to go.

"Don't worry," said Tarku's voice from the heap of bearskin on the floor. "It is just the tree machines. Very far away."

"What?" I stopped cramming the sleeping bag into my backpack and listened.

"The machines. They cut the trees down, but they are very far away. You don't need to worry."

"They sound like they're right there." I pointed.

"They're up there." A hand poked out of his furs and pointed toward the slope of the mountain. "It's the, what's your word? Echo."

I sat down again. "I should probably get going anyway," I said. "I need to work on finding a way out of here."

"You know," Tarku said. "I was thinking about that. I was thinking, what goes out of Grygia? And I think to myself, Logs! Logs go out of Grygia!"

"How do they go out?" I asked. I'd assumed they moved them by train.

"Steamtrucks. Big ones. Many, many of them a day. I don't know where they are going."

"They go everywhere," I told him. "Grygian lumber is famous. They use it for ships and houses. You may have a good idea there. If I could hide in the logs, I could get out of Grygia without anyone noticing." *And then, I could find a way to Simeria.*

He stood up and draped his bearskins around his shoulders again and tucked his sword into his belt. "Come on. I show you the way up to logging camp."

"This is how we not get caught," he told me as he showed me the network of bridges and Tree Dweller villages in the trees. It was incredible. Looking up at the dense canopy of trees, you would never have imagined that they contained a secret path through the forest, above the snow where our feet would leave footprints, above predators. We only had to come down from the trees a couple of times, when one community ended and there was a break of a quarter mile or so before the next one began. I pulled a bough down from a fir tree and used it to brush our prints away from the fresh snow.

As the sound of the giant logging machines got louder and louder, Tarku slowed down and chose our route carefully. We found a cluster of treehouses with an intact lookout post and scampered up the ladder to the little platform, hidden at the very top of the highest tree. The view was incredible from up here. We could see much of the wide Grygian valley and the mountains rising out of it.

"See," Tarku told me, pointing down to the camp. "Trucks are here to take logs out today."

He was right. A rough dirt road wound out from Gryg City toward the camp, and chugging along the road were two SteamTrucks, with long, covered beds for the logs. I could see men moving around, and there were two big SteamForkLifts that were getting ready to move a giant pile of logs.

Tarku watched the men moving around down below and said sadly, "That pile—it was the trees of at least five villages. Just gone."

"I'm sorry," I told him.

"Well, maybe you will help stop them, when you get where you are going. You have to hide behind that tree until they get the truck loaded and then you can sneak into it. Okay?"

"Okay," I said. "Thank you, Tarku, for everything. I hope you find your family. I hope you find your brother."

He just smiled and watched me climb down. When I was on the ground, I looked up, but he was lost amongst the trees.

I found a good hiding place behind a large stand of trees. The SteamTrucks rumbled into the camp and I watched as the drivers jumped out and started conferring with the men standing around. A group of Grygian Tree Dwellers was standing near the giant pile of logs, guarded by three BNDL agents. I stayed behind my tree and watched as the agents directed the Tree Dwellers to help load the logs on to the SteamLift. The Steam-

Lift hoisted them into the back of the truck and the Tree Dwellers jumped up and pushed them to the back.

Once the pile was gone and both trucks were loaded, the drivers got back into the cabs and the agents directed the Tree Dwellers to close up the back of the truck.

I was just starting to panic about how I was going to get into one of the trucks before they closed the back, when we heard a loud *whoop, whoop, whoop* from the other end of the camp. Someone, up in the trees, was shouting and drawing attention away from the trucks.

Tarku.

The agents all ran to see what was going on and once their backs were turned, I leapt up onto the back of the truck and climbed in amongst the logs. They were tightly packed, but there was a bit of space right at the back. Up against the Gryluminum wall of the truck. The side of the truck box was battered and there were a few holes that would ensure I would have some air and light.

A few minutes later, the back of the truck came down, the engines started up, and we were off.

For the next 24 hours, the truck bounced and bumped over the crude mountain roads that BNDL had built after the discovery of Grygia.

The trucks stopped twice, both times so the drivers could go to the bathroom. I ate and drank as little as I could from my stores, not knowing how long the journey would be. Finally, on the morning of the second day, the trucks stopped and I heard the drivers talking about having a meal. I watched out a little hole in the side of the truck, and when they disappeared inside a low building, I climbed over the logs, my backpack securely on my back, rolled up the back of the truck, and jumped out onto solid ground. It was very cold, so I zipped up my Explorer's vest, pulled my scarf up over my face and put on a thick wool hat and gloves. It was the perfect disguise. Everyone would be bundled up against the chill air. I didn't stop to look around.

It was early in the morning. The thin line of the pink sunrise showed in the eastern sky off to my right. I could see a mountain range over there and I kept it to my right as I headed toward Simeria.

light weight brass riveted goggles

customized wrench for steam engines

blue eyes

blonde straight hair

mechanic's cap

utilities

jump suit

cactus fiber T-shirt

EXPLORER'S VEST

Wicked fish knife

buffalo raw-hide belt

black cowhide EXPLORER LEGGINGS

old pair of Doolandian Buffalo leggings

tall brown cowhide boots

M.K.

Seven

I headed south however I could, taking trains and ferries, and hitching rides with farmers or fishermen. The sun became stronger as I went and I put away the thermal hat and gloves, and traded my fur-lined boots for a lighter suede pair I bought from a shepherd in southern Romania. I bought his baggy cotton trousers and white linen tunic too. I put my Explorer's vest into the backpack. I missed wearing it, but I needed to blend in, and in my shepherd's outfit, my face and arms tanned from days of walking in the sun, I passed as a local boy traveling to look for work.

I had a lot of time to think, and I spent most of that time on Blue Mask. Who was he? I didn't think he'd been sent by Mr. Mountmorris, so he must have been an Indorustan agent who knew I was working as a spy for BNDL and had been ordered to follow me. But how had he made his way across the border to Grygia and what did he want from me? Information? To stop me from finding Count von Rostovich's palace?

None of it made any sense, so I just closed my eyes and went to the place in my brain where I kept Dad's map of Simer City, alongside the ones I'd memorized in my training. I walked the streets, stopping at the places where the map in my head differed from the maps I'd found of the city.

When I got there, I'd be ready.

I had reached Greece when I made the mistake of taking a train during daylight hours. I'd been following a policy of only taking trains when I could board secretly and in the middle of the night, to avoid attracting the attention of the agents who had become very plentiful as I traveled near to the border. But I was getting closer—once I reached Athens, I'd take a ferry across the Mediterranean to Tyre and then to Simer City—and I convinced myself that it couldn't hurt to take the 11:00 AM Athens train.

Most of the journey was uneventful, but as we got closer, I started to suspect I had been trailed. I kept seeing things out of the corner of my eye, a flash of black disappearing behind a door as I made my way to the dining car, a shadow passing the crack in the lavatory door. That night, I awoke with a start, certain someone had been in my sleeping compartment, even though I checked and found the door locked from the inside.

The next day I was sitting in the dining car, eating a red pepper omelette, when I caught something moving in the corner of my vision. I looked up quickly and saw the back of a black-clad figure, wearing a blue balaclava, disappearing through the door. The train had stopped at a small country station and I knew I didn't have long if I was going to get off the train.

I made my way to the last car and ducked into the small lavatory, opening the window and sticking my head out to look up and down the tracks. There was no one to see me, so I dropped my backpack out the window, squeezed through behind it, and jumped down to the ground, and then I ducked behind a post holding up the tiny train station shelter.

I settled my pack onto my back and looked out at the empty platform. He hadn't followed me. I waited another ten seconds and then stepped out again, thinking I'd walk for a bit to let him get far away from this tiny, rural village.

But I didn't make it very far because Blue Mask, who must have been watching me from inside the train, suddenly launched himself from the open door and knocked me to the ground, pinning me to the pavement. Remembering my training, I tried to keep calm, reaching up into his coat pockets to see if I could find a convenient wallet. *Gather any information you can, any way you can, any time you can,* my Information Gathering instructor had told me. *Any interaction with another human being is an opportunity to learn something.*

No wallet, but my fingers closed around a scrap of paper.

I twisted away from him and leapt to my feet. I remembered practicing my roundhouse kick on a bag full of sawdust at the BNDL training facility. I bent my knees and came up with my leg extended, turning my body so that my leg made contact with his left shoulder.

Crunch.

It wasn't perfect—bags of sawdust don't move when you kick them—but it did the job. Blue Mask fell to the ground, looking stunned. I straddled him and met his eyes. Up close they were brown and widened in fear.

"Why are you following me?" I demanded.

He just stared at me and didn't say anything.

The train was starting to move and I knew I had to let him go. I sprinted toward the tracks and leapt back onto a middle car, slipping through the door and watching out the window as Blue Mask got to his feet and tried to run after the train. But he wasn't fast enough and as we gathered speed, I saw him fall behind.

Had he been following me ever since Gryg City? If he had, he must have a pretty good sense now of where I'd been heading.

I smiled, watching his confusion, and unfolded the piece of paper I'd taken from his coat pocket.

It was covered with notes written in Russian, times and places scrawled in blue pencil. At the very bottom were five words written in English:

The Lost City of Maps.

I read them again, smiling. I was one step ahead now and I was going to make sure I stayed that way.

In Athens, I caught a ferry that would take me to Tyre, where I would travel to Simer City by SteamTrain. I bought my ticket hours ahead of time and hid myself behind a pile of fish crates on the dock, watching everyone who boarded. I snuck on at the very last minute so I could be positive no one had followed me.

It was warmer now, and standing on deck and looking out across the endless blue of the Mediterranean, I closed my eyes to the sun and imagined the ancient streets, imagining too the sounds and smells of the desert.

I was almost there.

I finished the book Marek had given me. There was a lot I didn't know about Simeria. The legends said that Simer City had been a crossroads of the busy ancient world, but that it had been lost to time, buried beneath the violent sandstorms that plagued the region. The book talked about a place called The Lost City of Maps near Simer City, where there was an ancient library that held incredible collections of books and maps. The legends said that it too had been lost to time, and the book said that even after the discovery of Simer City by the Explorer Akhbar El Alton, the legend of the Lost City of Maps remained just that. In the meantime, though, Simeria had become an important territory for the United States and Allied Nations.

The western part of the territory around the Simer River was in a rich, fertile valley and the Simerian Territories provided much of the produce for the Allied nations in that part of the world—or at least they had before the uprisings.

The northern and eastern part of the Simerian Territories, however, was a vast desert, plagued by violent sandstorms, and much of it was unmapped.

Which is where I came in.

Mr. Mountmorris had someone watching me, so I couldn't spend too long in Simer City before setting off across the desert. Four or five days might seem reasonable. I had a lot to do. I needed to explore the city to see if I could figure out the secret to Dad's map. At the same time, I had to appear as though I was getting ready for my expedition into the desert, in case someone was watching. And I needed to figure out who Blue Mask was and why he was following me.

I opened my eyes and looked out across the water. A faint wind moved over my face and in the far, far distance, I thought I could make out a thin line of beige.

As soon as I arrived in Tyre, I boarded a SteamTrain making its way to Simer City. Outside the train windows, the scrubby land flashed by, turning to desert as we traveled east.

I was almost there.

Eight

I arrived in Simer City on a cloudless morning, three weeks after I'd left Grygia. It was February 1st. The train station was noisy and hot. Men unloaded crates and boxes from the train, and a woman dressed in long red robes and lots of silver jewelry sold iced mint teas from a cart. A girl led three camels past the station to the excited shouts of a group of children waiting around to see something interesting.

The desert stretched out around the city in every direction, rolling dunes of sand to the east, a beige expanse dotted with green to the west, and ahead of me, the unmistakable walls of Old Simer City.

No one seemed very interested in a boy wearing a simple canvas backpack, walking alone off the Tyre train. I was wearing a light tunic I'd bought from a boy in Tyre and a white scarf wrapped around my head the way he'd shown me. He'd explained that it was good for keeping the sun off my head. It was good for helping me blend in too.

I checked twice to make sure I hadn't been followed and then hiked up the hill from the station and stood beneath the Snake's Gate at the western entrance to the old city. A large snake's head emerged from the arch at the top of the gate, its tongue sticking out, its eyes narrowed and menacing. Smaller versions of the snake's head decorated either side of the gate, where it connected with the high wall around the city.

I walked beneath the archway, feeling a bit of the nervousness and awe that ancient invading armies might have felt approaching the city. For many years, the city walls and the sandstorms had kept the city safe from those armies.

But at some point in history, the city had been abandoned and the sandstorms had covered it until Akhbar El Alton had discovered its ruins.

Modern Simer City had been built on top of the

ancient city and the effect was strange—old cobblestone streets winding next to more modern ones, crumbled columns lying amongst the grid of metal and glass buildings, and new sandstone buildings made to look old. The old wall was still standing and it wound its way all around the city.

Once it was discovered how fertile the land was west of the city, in a protected valley where the sandstorms couldn't wreak too much havoc, people had flocked to Simer City from all over the region. It was known for the many religions that coexisted peacefully, and as I looked down the ancient cobblestone streets, I could see the dome of the Old Mosque in the very center of the city, along with churches, temples, more mosques, and the meeting houses of the Mappists and the Neo-Creationists, side-by-side with shops and BNDL office buildings. I had read that over one hundred languages were spoken in the city, though English, Arabic, and Russian were most common.

It was only ten in the morning, but already the sun was searing over my head. I needed to carefully trace the streets, matching them to the map in my head. But first, I needed something to eat and drink.

I found a little café in the old city and was just about

to sit down at one of the outdoor tables when I noticed a sign announcing the large tan-colored building across the street as Simer City's main post office.

I hesitated. I had told Sukey to write if she was in trouble or something was wrong. But she was probably too busy with Zander and her training.

Still, what if something had happened? I decided to check, just to be sure. The post office's lobby was busy and I had to wait in a long line at the counter. My stomach growled with hunger and sweat poured down my back. When I finally made it to the counter, my tunic was almost completely soaked.

"How can I help you?" asked the exhausted-looking woman behind the counter in Simerian.

"Yes, um, do you have a letter for Yoren Balloty, by any chance?" I asked in Simerian, and I tried to keep my voice down, in case any agents were listening.

She turned away, scanning a shelf behind her. "No, nothing. Sorry," she said.

"Oh, okay. Thanks." The disappointment hit me like a punch to the chest. I'd known Sukey wouldn't write unless it was an emergency. Why had I let myself hope?

I was almost out the door when the woman called out, "Mr. Balloty? I am very sorry. It fell down on the floor!"

I went back and took the long brown envelope from her, my heart hammering in my chest. I recognized Sukey's handwriting and the Grygian stamp.

Casually, in case someone was watching, I tucked it into my vest, which I'd put on under my tunic, and went back to the café. I found a table and ordered iced tea and what seemed to be the local specialty of grilled meat with chopped vegetables and bread. I ate more than I was really hungry for, and drank all of the sweet mint tea, and then, making sure no one was watching me, I opened the envelope and took out a letter.

My dear Yoren,

It has been a long time since we have written to you. Mother is quite sick and we are out of money. The cow has died and the goat is very sick. I have been trying to make some extra money by plucking the dog's fur and knitting it into hats. Perhaps we will soon have some food to eat.

I hope that you are well and that you are still alive.

Love, your sister, Ludmilla

I smiled. "Ludmilla" was really laying it on thick. The letter might have been quite alarming if I hadn't understood what Sukey had done. I hunched over, in case anyone was watching, and carefully peeled the top layer of the letter away, revealing another thin sheet underneath.

Dear Kit:

I hope this letter makes it to you. The agents on base have been watching me all the time and I had to get one of the cooks to mail the letter for me. I bet they'll open it, but I don't think they'll be able to figure out the secret. Tomorrow, we leave for Simeria. M.K. is doing great. They've had her building things for them and she seems happy.

Zander seems very worried. They've had him off in strategy meetings with Leo Nackley and Foley, and Joyce told me that they're expecting a lot of him, maybe even putting him in charge of some part of a possible invasion.

That's the main thing I wanted to tell you. It looks like they're planning for an an invasion and I think it's going to be in the next few months. Wherever you are and whatever you're doing, try to stay safe, okay? We'll be heading for the ADR base in Simer City in two days. Take care and I'll look for you when I get there.

Yours, Sukey

I checked the date of the letter. Two weeks ago. She might already be in Simeria. I reread it.

Yours, Sukey. It wasn't *Love, Sukey*, but it felt like something.

Yours, Sukey.

I told myself not to be an idiot, tucked it back inside my vest and finished the rest of my tea.

"You like it?" my waiter asked in Simerian.

I told him I did.

"Drink lots of tea today. It's going to be hot," he said. "Good day for the parade."

"What parade?"

"It's February 1st. Discovery Day. Big military parade this afternoon. You should go."

"I will," I told him. Encouraged by his friendliness, I asked him, "What would you use to travel in the desert? Camels?" I handed over five Allied dollars for my meal.

"Some like camels," he said. "They are slow, but they don't need much water. The Europeans like horses. Horses are fast and can be better in the sandstorms, but they need lots of water and food. Risky. The Ottomanland traders like the Giant Dab Lizards, and the traders from the north like Tiker Horses. But Tiker Horses can be nasty. They only like the person who trained them to ride."

He seemed to be thinking deeply. "Me? I would probably go with a camel," he said finally. "All things considered."

I thanked him, checked again to make sure no one had tailed me and, following the map in my head, started to explore Old Simer City.

Nine

It was a strange experience being in a city for the first time but knowing its streets and avenues as though I'd lived there my whole life. The map I'd seen on the wall of the temple in King Triton's Lair, the one branded on the surface of my brain now, had shown a rectangular walled city, with four gates, one on each side of the rectangle. The streets on the map in my head spiralled in towards the center in a distinctive labrynthine pattern; that pattern was what had made me recognize it as a map of Simer City. The map I'd seen on the wall in the temple in King Triton's Lair had shown the carved animal heads that distinguished each of the four gates to the city. At the southern entrance gate was a leopard, at the eastern gate a dragon, at the northern gate a lion, and at the western gate, the snake's head, which I'd already seen.

The cobbled sandstone streets were almost empty; I knew that most residents of the city were probably inside, resting during the hottest part of the day. I was in a full sweat, my tunic soaked underneath my backpack. I would have liked to be inside too. But I didn't have any time to waste.

I followed the street that wrapped around the wall and approached the northern entrance to the city, ready to see the Lion's Gate that was there on the map in my head. But when I reached the northern gate, I found that it had the head of a leopard carved into it, rather than the lion I'd been expecting. I checked again and searched my memory. I was right. The map I'd seen in King Triton's Lair had definitely shown the Lion's Gate at the northern entrance.

It took me nearly an hour to follow the wall around to the eastern Dragon Gate and then down to the southern gate. Just as I'd been expecting, there was a lion where I'd been expecting a leopard.

So this was the Lion Gate.

It appeared that the map in King Triton's Lair was wrong.

I stood there for a moment in the sun, carrying on a silent conversation with myself while the city woke up around me.

But Dad's maps are never wrong.

Dad may not have made the King Triton's map.

But he wanted you to see it. He wanted you to come to Simer City.

Why?

I stood there looking at the Lion Gate and even inspected the stone archway and walls, trying to see if there was any clue to the gate's significance. There were smaller carved lions all over the walls, but there was nothing obvious to tell me what Dad had wanted me notice.

I needed to know more.

It was now early afternoon. A lot of the streets were blocked off by military vehicles—for the parade, I assumed—and I had to walk an extra half-mile or so to get back to the old city and the market.

I ordered fruit and tea at another café and sat against the wall, watching the streets, not trying to keep myself out of sight this time. I wanted to know if Blue Mask had followed me. And if Marek had made it all the way to Simeria, I wanted him to be able to approach me without getting caught.

There were agents and soldiers everywhere, eating at the cafés, standing on the corners, talking to merchants in the marketplace. As I ate, I thought about the map. I had assumed that when I got to Simer City, I'd figure out why Dad wanted me to come here.

But now that I was here, I felt even more in the dark.

I knew that Dad didn't make mistakes on his maps. But he hadn't made the map in King Triton's Lair. Someone else had.

He *had* wanted me to see it, though, I reminded myself. Though it was different from the other maps, he had, in a sense, left it for me. And it was different from the actual map of Simer City in two very specific ways.

So that had to mean something.

Maybe the map in my head wasn't of Simer City at all, but of a nearly identical city that was important for some reason.

But what city? What if I was in the wrong place completely.

I felt my heart sink.

There was nothing to do now but figure out how I was going to get out to Count Von Rostovich's palace in the desert. Mr. Mountmorris said that he had people watching me and I needed to convince whoever they were that I was preparing for my mission like a good little spy. I headed towards the stalls where I'd seen the horse and camel merchants displaying their animals. The streets were filling with people holding U.S. and Simerian flags and I could see soldiers and children dressed in bright red and holding Simerian flags lining up in the side streets. Somewhere a band was practicing a jaunty marching anthem.

Just off Simer Avenue, a crowd of kids was holding up a big sign reading, "Tour the Famous Underground caves of Simer City! Learn about the History of Simeria. Only 2 Allied Dollars!"

"Come on!" the kids shouted at me. "Only two dollars!"

"All right, all right," I told them as they crowded around me and pulled me toward a hole in the ground with a ladder poking out of it.

I paid the kids and they pointed to the ladder. I climbed down into it and two of the boys followed, holding torches made of rags soaked in oil and wrapped around what looked like a baseball bat. Once we were below ground, I could see a series of rooms that had been dug out of the earth.

"What was this used for?" I asked the boys.

95

"This is where people lived, many years ago, in the ancient city," the boy told me in Simerian. "When they got attacked, they hid down here."

I wandered around the dark network of rooms. The boys told me about how it was believed that the ancient people of Simer City had created the caves to hide from invaders. In more recent times, travelers had found the caves and used them to shelter from the sandstorms. The boys had made little handwritten signs, showing where families had slept and had fires and created holes in the ceiling for sunlight to poke through.

The older of the two boys spoke excellent English and he showed me a series of black hieroglyphs and letters and stick figures on the walls, explaining that they told the stories of invasions and wars, and listed the names of ancient Simerians who had lived in the caves.

"Once, there were tunnels to the desert," one boy said. "I have heard stories about it. Secret tunnels. But no more. No one has seen tunnels for many, many years."

"That would be handy, wouldn't it, to be able to avoid the sandstorms?" I said.

"Yes, but the tunnels are all filled in now."

"Are you sure?"

"Yes." He smiled at the other boy. "We have been in

all the caves. There are no more tunnels. All filled in."
It was dark and dank and I felt claustrophobic all of a
sudden. I tried to imagine what it would have been like to
live down here for years.

I was wandering around, looking at the drawings on
the walls, when a word jumped out at me. "What does
this say?" I asked the boy. "*Kharasina*. That's the Simerian word for map, right?"

"Uh, maps," he said. "It says they come from the
maps of the… the city of maps. Something like that. It's
hard to read. Oh, it must be the Lost City of Maps."

"Are you sure? The Lost City of Maps?" I tried to
keep my voice calm. I didn't want him to know how
excited I was. "What is that? What does that mean?"

"The Lost City of Maps is like a legend. I remember
my mother telling me stories about the heroes who look
for it. It's way out in the desert, where the sandstorms
are. The heroes in the stories are always lost."

"An ancient city? Like Simer City?"

"Well yes," the boy said. "In fact, it was supposed to
be a twin city, exactly the same as Simer City, but it was
called the Lost City of Maps."

A twin city. A city the same as—or almost the same
as—Simer City. But in the desert.

"Do you think it's just a story?" I asked him.

"Well, if it's real, no one's ever been able to find it because it's in the Simerian Desert," he said. "It's impossible to get there."

"Thank you," I told the boys. "I don't think you have any idea how grateful I am to you."

The parade was in full swing by the time I climbed back to the surface and I stood for a moment in the harsh sunlight, listening to the music a few streets over before I headed for the markets.

The day felt suddenly full of energy and promise. Now I knew what I needed to do.

The Lost City of Maps.

A twin city to Simer City. Out in the desert. *Another ancient city with the same layout as Simer City. Or almost the same layout.*

Another ancient city with the same layout as the map Dad had left for me in King Triton's Lair.

I was willing to bet my life that the twin city, the one out in the desert, was the city Dad had wanted me to find.

Now I just had to get there.

Ten

In order to get back to the market and avoid the parade, I cut through a series of side streets and alleyways, thinking about what I'd learned. I was pretty sure I now knew what Dad had wanted me to find in Simeria, and it was a stroke of luck that it was in the same place where Mr. Mountmorris had sent me on my mission.

Or was it?

I was lost in thought as I walked, which was why I didn't hear the footsteps behind me until they were very close.

I wheeled around.

We were in a narrow blind alley ending in someone's front door. Sheets fluttered on a laundry line above us and at the end of the alley stood a now familiar figure. Blue Mask. There wasn't anywhere for me to hide, so I fumbled at my belt for my knife and held it out in front of me. "Who are you?" I asked him. "Why are you following me? What do you want?"

He didn't say anything. The mask covered most of his face, but instead of the warm coat, he was wearing a lightweight tunic and pants like mine. I jabbed the knife at the air, but he kept coming, his hands out in front of him. It was unnerving, not being able to see his face at all. I jabbed at the air with the knife again. "Don't come any closer," I shouted. "Why are you following me?"

He didn't say a word, just kept walking. Finally, my training kicked in and I bent my knees, ready to launch myself at him. He didn't stop, so I kicked out once, to throw him off balance and then when he started to counter with a kick of his own, I threw myself forward and knocked him to the cobblestones.

"Who are you?" I demanded again.

I don't know how, but he shifted his weight slightly

and suddenly I was being rolled over. He straddled me, pinning my arms to the ground.

"Let me go!" I said as I struggled with him. "I just want to talk to you."

He didn't say a word. I kept struggling but I couldn't free my hands.

I could hear the beating of drums and voices singing over on Simer Avenue, but there was no one near enough to hear me. "Let me go," I said again. I recognized his wide brown eyes behind the mask.

Finally, I let my body go limp and when he let up the pressure on my arms, I struggled out of his grasp and got to my feet. We were both crouching on the pavement now, "Why are you following me?" I asked again. His eyes narrowed.

I may have imagined it, but I almost thought he was going to answer my question when he turned toward a blur of motion next to him. Suddenly a figure appeared behind him, holding a rock high in the air. He brought it down against the side of Blue Mask's head.

Blue Mask groaned and slumped over, but then found the strength to reach out and push the new arrival down before lurching away from us toward the other end of the alley, disappearing around the corner.

I scrambled to my feet, but he was already gone and I turned around to see who had saved me.

The newcomer's face was wrapped in a brown scarf, but he reached up to unwind it. "You don't have to thank me," he said in a familiar voice. "You're welcome. Oh, and 'My sister's cat just had six kittens.'"

He smiled. My surprise must have been emblazoned across my face.

It was Kemal Asker.

Eleven

I waited until we had put a few streets between us and Blue Mask before I stopped and said, "*You're* the agent who's here to help me?" At the ends of the side streets, we could see the parade making its way along Simer Avenue and we could hear the music getting louder and louder.

Kemal grinned. "Yeah. I can't believe you didn't guess before now. I was sure you'd figured it out when we were in the Caribbean."

"But…" I had so many questions I didn't know where to start. "How long have you been assigned to protect me?"

"Since not long after you arrived at the Academy. Mr. Mountmorris asked me to keep an eye on you." He looked up at me guiltily. "I said I didn't want to spy on you, but he said he only wanted me to make sure you were safe. He said that because of your father, there were people who might want to hurt you. My job was to stay close and come to your aid if you needed it."

I stared at him. Could he really have believed that Mr. Mountmorris just wanted him to keep me safe? Or was he just saying that so that I wouldn't know he was there to spy on me?

"How long have you known I was coming here?" I asked him.

"Just since Gryg City, the morning after you were supposedly sent home."

I watched him, trying to figure out if he was telling the truth or not. He seemed relaxed, meeting my eyes and smiling easily. "What happened that night?" I wanted to ask how Sukey was and what she thought about my disappearance but I couldn't.

"It was crazy. There was a fire and then it turned into this huge fight. The agents had to come in and arrest the Tree Dwellers. Mr. Mountmorris told everyone that you had assaulted Leo Nackley and he'd disciplined you and sent you home on a commercial airship."

"The assault part is actually true," I told him. "He followed me and I had to do something."

"Well, it worked. Everyone thinks you're already back in New York. I bought it until Mr. Mountmorris called me in and told me to follow you and help you out if necessary."

"Like that," I said.

"Like that. Now that my cover's blown, I'm supposed to come along on your mission."

"Are you… are you sure?"

"That's what Mr. Mountmorris said."

I tried to ignore the sense of panic that washed over me. How was I going to figure out why Dad had sent me to the Lost City of Maps if Kemal was along for the expedition into the desert? Somehow, I was going to have to figure out how to lose him.

"I don't need you to come," I said. "It's going to be hard enough to complete my mission alone. If there are two of us, it's going to be even harder."

Kemal just stared at me.

"What?" I didn't meet his eyes.

"You really think that *you're* going to be able to find a convincing cover story? I'd say my chances are a bit better since I actually look like I could live here. I think you need me."

"But…" There was no way I could stop him from coming without alerting Mr. Mountmorris that I had another mission. "All right, Kemal. Thank you."

"And of course you're the expedition leader," he told me. "I'm just here to protect you from things like *that* happening again."

"Who *was* that anyway?" I asked him. "Do you have any ideas?"

"I don't know, but whoever it is he's been following you since Gryg City. I just barely caught up to him."

I stared at him. "So, you've been following me this whole time?"

"Well, yes, although I lost you for a long time. I wasn't sure where you went after the fight in the Tree Dweller village, but I checked all the routes out of Grygia and when I heard a load of logs had gone out two days later, I figured it was a good bet. I got a ride with a trucker and got lucky. I saw you climb out of the truck at that restaurant and followed you. I lost you and then found you again when you got off the ferry in Tyre.

Whoever the guy in the blue mask is, he's been here for a couple of days."

"He must have been waiting for me."

"What do you think he wants?" Kemal asked.

I wasn't sure whether I should tell him about Blue Mask's interest in the Lost City of Maps. Could I trust him?

I decided to wait before saying anything more.

"He must be an Indorustan agent," I said. "That's the only explanation."

"So what do we do now?" Kemal asked.

"How much do you know about my mission?"

"Mountmorris said it was on a need-to-know basis," he told me. "He said you'd tell me as much as you could once I'd made myself known to you."

"Okay," I said, keeping my voice down. "There's this guy who lives way out in the Simerian desert. His name is Count Grigory von Rostovich. No one's ever been out there because of the sandstorms. But we need to find his palace and steal his maps."

We had to step out of the way to avoid colliding with an old woman pushing a cart full of chickens on the sidewalk.

When I looked back at Kemal, his eyes were wide and he was staring at me as though I'd gone insane.

"Oh, is that all?" he asked, his voice dripping with sarcasm. "No problem then."

I turned to look at him. He wasn't smiling. "You don't understand. When my family escaped from Ottoman-land, we went five hundred miles out of our way to avoid the Simerian Desert. It's impossible to cross. There's a reason no one has ever mapped it."

"So you think Mr. Mountmorris is sending us on a suicide mission?"

"I don't know, but I'm telling you, it's impossible to cross. The only ones who know how to avoid the sand-storms are the traders, but they don't share their secrets with anyone. I've heard rumors that they have secret charts that show the times when it's safe to cross, but no one's ever seen them. They—what's wrong?"

"Nothing, I just thought I heard Mr. Mountmorris's voice."

Kemal pointed to the end of the street where the parade was passing. "You don't think…?"

"Come on. We can't let anyone see us, though."

We made our way to the end of the side street and hid behind a stack of orange crates piled up against a bright blue door to watch the parade pass by.

Rows of soldiers dressed in the red uniforms of the

Simerian Defense Force marched by, each of them carrying an ornamental sword. They were followed by Allied Defense Force soldiers.

"Wave to our brave men and women in uniform," boomed Mr. Mountmorris's voice, as the soldiers marched by. From where we were hiding, I couldn't see him. But I'd know his voice anywhere.

"And now," Mr. Mountmorris called out. "Let's welcome our trainee officers from the Academy for the Exploratory Sciences. They have just arrived in Simer City to help to defend this great land."

Kemal pushed me back against the door as though he was afraid I was going to run out. We both watched as Lazlo Nackley and Jack Foster walked by. I thought I saw the back of Zander's head, but I couldn't be sure.

Leo Nackley walked by, waving at the crowd, grinning his fake grin.

And then suddenly, a line of boys and girls in green flight suits came into view. I caught a quick glimpse of Sukey's copper hair as she turned this way and that, waving at the crowds.

She was right there. They all were. But there was nothing I could do about it.

As soon as Sukey was gone from my sight, I stood up.

"We have to get out of Simer City before someone recognizes us," I told Kemal. I took some money out of my vest and handed it over to him. "You go buy the food we'll need for the journey and figure out where we can get some water bags and fill them up. I'll look into our transportation. Wrap your scarf around your face in case someone sees you." I wrapped my own scarf around the lower part of my face.

Kemal watched me for a moment before he took the money. "You're the boss, but I'm telling you, it's impossible. If we don't get lost in a sandstorm, we'll get killed by the traders who want to protect their routes. We should at least try to find out when the sandstorms are the most intense."

I glanced toward Simer Avenue. The parade would be breaking up any minute now and everyone would stream into the market. There were at least twenty or thirty people in the city who would recognize us. "We don't have time, Kemal."

He hesitated, but nodded. I told him I would meet him in an hour.

At one end of the market was a makeshift stable, a long low building with room for the horses and camels that traders used to travel. Men were walking up and down the rows, bargaining for the tired-looking animals. I saw a couple of odd, striped animals that I figured were Tiker Horses and a large stall filled with Giant Dab Lizards. The lizards were as big as ponies, with greeny beige scales and large, intelligent brown eyes and spines along their necks and tails. They were fitted with elegant leather saddles and harnesses, and when I stopped in front of their stall, they made little clicking sounds, as though they were trying to talk to me.

The camels chewed hay and watched me as I walked by. Next to the camels were two beautiful black Arabian stallions. I imagined myself riding across the desert on one of them, the golden sand dunes rippling all around me.

I asked the man who owned the horses how much they cost and he quoted a price that was five times that of the camels.

Kemal and I wouldn't look as cool riding across the desert on a pair of camels, but we could afford them.

I told the man I wanted to think about it and wandered along the rows of vendors in the market, weighing the merits of camels and horses.

There were rug merchants, selling beautiful rugs woven from vibrant reds and blues and greens. I saw one that I knew Raleigh would have loved and told myself I'd get it for him when I came back from the desert.

If I came back from the desert.

I finished arranging our transportation and then, my scarf up around my face, I waved Kemal over when I spotted him across the market. He was wearing a backpack that looked quite full now and he was carrying two huge goatskin bags that could be filled with water.

"I think I got everything," he said. "There's a place to get water at the other end of the market, but we should wait until we know how we're traveling. Do we know how we're traveling?"

"Yes, but it's a surprise," I told him. "Follow me."

We had arrived back at the horse and camel stalls. A tall camel wearing a saddle reached out and nibbled on my ear.

"Did you buy a camel?"

"Not exactly."

"Horses?"

"Not really."

I led him down a narrow alley behind the stables.

Tied to the fence and waiting for me to come back were thirteen Giant Dab Lizards. The two largest lizards were outfitted with leather saddles and saddlebags.

"Meet Bob and Andrew," I told Kemal. I reached out to stroke the chin of one the Giant Dab Lizards. Andrew made his funny clicking sound and Bob licked him with his long blue tongue.

"Kemal, you are now the son of a highly successful Giant Dab Lizard dealer from Ottomanland, traveling across the desert to sell these lizards to Count von Rostovich. And I," I wrapped the headscarf more tightly around my head and smiled, "am your cousin."

Kemal raised his eyebrows.

"You know, I've always wanted to ride a Giant Dab Lizard across the Simerian desert," he said.

"That's funny," I said, leading the lizards out of the stable, the eleven lizards for sale tied to Bob and Andrew's saddles. We secured the water bags and swung on to the lizards' backs. They clicked and whistled and we set off towards the desert. "So have I."

square-rimmed glasses

Yak-fiber sweater-lined with Namwee fur

cactus fiber T-shirt

map

dark hair

looks like Mom

navy eyes

EXPLORER'S VEST

utilities

arm guards

brass compass

gloves

Dad's alligator skin leggings

back pack with secret compartment

tall brown cowhide boots with hidden crampons

black cowhide EXPLORER LEGGINGS

KIT

Twelve

We rode as far as the Eastern Simerian Territories that night, bedding down at a small boarding house that seemed to be mostly inhabited by migrant farmers. With all of the unrest, many of the farm owners had left Simeria and their crops, so the migrant workers had moved in, claiming parts of the farms for themselves, working the fields and selling what they could.

A boy about our age was serving up bowls of spicy beef stew for two dollars each, and Kemal and I had firsts and seconds, as well as two slices of the boy's homemade almond cake.

"You're a really good cook, you know," I told him. "You could have an actual restaurant in the city if you wanted."

"Thanks." He grinned. "But I'm heading north next week. There's going to be an invasion soon and I don't think the Indorustans will appreciate my cooking quite as much as you do."

"What makes you think the invasion's coming?" Kemal asked.

"There are lots of rumors about it," the boy said. "People say there are more spies than ever." He lowered his voice. "That guy over there is a spy, I think." He nodded to a man with gray hair and a moustache sitting at a table on the other side of the room. He *did* look like a spy.

But then, Kemal and I were spies too, I realized, smiling a little at the thought.

"By the way," the boy told us. "I wouldn't leave your lizards out there all night. This place is full of thieves."

"Thanks. And good luck," I told him.

We took his advice; Kemal kept watch the first part of the night and then I let him have the flea-ridden cot we'd rented for the second part.

We headed into the desert as soon as it got light.

I didn't know much about Giant Dab Lizards—actually, I didn't know *anything* about Giant Dab Lizards—but we soon got a sense of their funny personalities. They were as friendly as dogs, stretching their long scaly necks to rub their heads against our hands when we dismounted for a water break. They moved fast, galloping across the ground as Kemal and I clung to the long, curved saddle horns. The rest of the herd deferred to Andrew and Bob, following along behind them through the desert and watching to see what the bigger lizards were doing. For each lizard, we'd packed two saddlebags full of dried meat and just before we left, we'd given them what the dealer said was half a day's ration and watched them tear the meat apart with their sharp teeth.

The fertile farmland just outside Simer City gave way to a different landscape—not desert yet, but scrubby bushes and plants growing out of loose beige soil that became sandier and sandier the farther east we traveled. In the distance we could see mountains and a shimmery haze of sand.

We rode for half the day then stopped to eat lunch and rest the lizards. Under the bright sun, we snacked on bread and cheese, and had a few small sips of the water we'd brought. Water was heavy and necessary. We needed to ration it carefully.

We kept riding and by 2:00 PM we were in the real desert. The sun was hot overhead and I was glad to have the white scarf wrapped around my head and face to provide some protection. I quickly saw how easy it would be to get lost out here. Everything looked the same, and the heat created strange shimmering mirages. Off to the west were the Simerian mountains, but the silhouette of the range changed as we went, shapeshifting depending on the light and our perspective.

We continued north by Dad's old compass and though I was bored and a bit edgy the first couple of hours, I eventually settled into Bob's predictable rhythm and even napped a bit as the day wore on. We were moving so fast it was impossible for Kemal and I to carry on a conversation, and though it added to my boredom, I found that I was glad. I still didn't know how much to tell him about my mission. Mr. Mountmorris had said that whomever he sent to help me would be trustworthy, but he hadn't said how much I should reveal. And then there was my other mission. I still didn't know how I was going to look for the Lost City of Maps in the middle of the desert with Kemal there every second to make sure I was okay.

We stopped for the night as the sun dropped towards the edge of the desert. There was no shelter; in fact there was nothing to distinguish one patch of sand from another, so while we could still see, we just stopped. We fed Bob and Andrew and the other lizards, and watched as they dug shallow holes in the sand and settled down for the night. As soon as the sun was gone, it started to get cold and we could see why the lizards liked to bury themselves in a blanket of sand. I'd asked about desert travel conditions and had purchased some thin, plant fiber blankets that Kemal and I huddled under while we ate more bread and cheese. We had some chickpeas, and lots of crackers and dried fish to eat once the bread and cheese were gone. We didn't know if we'd be offered any food at Count von Rostovich's Palace—we didn't know if we'd even make it there much less get inside— and I remembered what I'd learned about food rationing and survival hunting in desert environments.

I lay down next to Bob, wrapping my blanket around me and using his left leg as a pillow, and Kemal did the same with Andrew. The lizards snored a little, making clucking sounds in their sleep that made me think of our parrot Pucci. It was comforting to have them there. It would be hard for anything to sneak up on us in the desert, and I was pretty sure Bob and Andrew would alert us if anything tried.

"Look at the stars," Kemal said. The sky was a blueblack dome above us, the stars, points on a graph that neither of us could complete.

"They seem so close." I searched and found familiar constellations, Canis Major and Lepus and Camelopardalis.

"When we first came to the United States, that was the thing that seemed strangest to me out of all the strange things. That they were the same stars we saw at home," Kemal said. "Here they are again. The same ones."

"Not the same stars my Dad can see in Fazia, though." I said it quietly, without really thinking.

There was a long silence.

"You think he's still alive, don't you?" Kemal asked me.

I decided to be honest. If he wanted to tell Mr. Mountmorris, then let him.

"I know he is," I said. "And I'm going to find him."

"You know…" He sighed and looked up at the stars again.

"What?" I asked him.

"Nothing, just… I'll help you, if I can. When the time comes."

"Thanks, Kemal."

We slept surprisingly well, waking up to the Dab Lizards licking our faces and the sun peeking up over the horizon. We drank some water, gave a bit to the lizards, who didn't need much, thanks to their ability to store it in their broad tails, and finished off the bread before swinging up into the saddles and starting off again for another day of riding across the monotonous desert. I was starting to understand why it drove people crazy. There was something about the sameness of it, the lack of any distinguishing features, that made you lose all track of time and space. Only the compass told us we were going in the right direction.

I started to have a strange feeling in the afternoon, a small, insistent buzzing telling me something was different. It may just have been that I was picking up on the lizards' nervousness, because about an hour after I first felt my brain go into high alert, they started swinging their heads from side to side, as though they were looking for someone… or something.

I shouted to Kemal and when he turned around to look at me, I could see that he was nervous too. I grabbed the reins and pulled Bob to a halt. "What do you think it is?" I called to him.

"I don't know. It could be an animal," he called back. "Should we rest for a bit?"

I shook my head. "Let's keep going." Whatever it was, I figured we were safer on lizardback than we were on the ground.

We kept on riding into the endless horizon of beige space.

And then, around three o'clock, I saw something on the horizon.

At first I thought what I was seeing up ahead must be my imagination, and I remembered hearing stories of people lost in the desert who thought they could see water or cities or beautiful gardens. The heat made everything shimmer and move and little specks appeared and then resolved themselves into nothing.

But the dark shapes I saw up ahead did not go away and after an hour or so, I shouted to Kemal to stop and asked him if he could see them too.

He peered out from under the scarf wrapped around his head and face. "Maybe." He didn't sound that convinced so we kept going.

But the dark shapes got bigger and finally Kemal

stopped me. "You're right," he said. "It looks to me like camels. Lots of them. I think they're coming from the northwest. Our paths will cross at some point up there."

"Traders?" I remembered the stories about the traders and how protective they were of their routes across the desert.

"I'd say Simerian bedouins. There are so many of them. It's probably a whole family. They move across the desert in big groups, looking for water and game."

There wasn't anything to do but to keep going, and sure enough, after another hour of travel, the small shapes resolved themselves into a caravan of camels, each with one or more people on their backs, and heavily laden with fabric-wrapped bundles and parcels.

It was strange, watching them approach us for such a long time. Then finally they were there. A man, his face and head wrapped in a scarf like mine, pulled the scarf away from his face and shouted a greeting as he passed. I didn't understand the word, but I shouted a hello back. Kemal and I pulled up the lizards and we watched them pass, probably thirty men, women and children, all wrapped against the sun and all shouting the same word at us.

We must have stared back stupidly enough that they

realized we didn't know what they were saying because as the last couple of camels went by, the children began to wave their hands in the air, shouting the word to us again.

It was the last of them, a little boy sitting behind an older girl, who finally made us understand.

He waved his hands in the air and then, searching for the words he must have heard from an English-speaking trader at some point in his young life, he shouted something that made me stop Bob in his tracks.

"Sandstorm!"

Thirteen

"There's nothing we can do," Kemal told me. "We need to just keep riding. If we can get to Count von Rostovich's palace, maybe there will be somewhere near there we can shelter."

"Okay." There *wasn't* anything else we could do, of course. The night before, the lack of trees or buildings or anywhere to hide had been comforting. Nothing was going to sneak up on us without us knowing. But now it was the lack of anything else in this whole wide wasteland of a place that seemed so sinister.

There was nowhere to hide.

Bob and Andrew seemed okay, which I took to be a

good sign. The lizards must have been able to sense that a sandstorm was coming. At least they would let us know.

We rode on, the red sunset to our left, and decided to keep going through the night in case we had a chance of reaching the palace.

I put my Explorer's vest on over my robes and turned on the light on my vest. Bob and I led the way, galloping across the dark sand into the night.

I was so tired; all I wanted to do was sleep, but Mr. Mountmorris's story about the operative and his horse kept echoing in my head and I kept digging my heels into Bob's side when I sensed he was slowing down. I called out to Kemal every once in a while to make sure he was behind me.

We rode all through the night; the sky was just beginning to lighten when we heard something, a far-off hissing that grew quickly louder.

"Keep going," I shouted to Kemal.

He nodded his head and shouted something, but I couldn't hear what he said.

Ahead of us, in the east, the sun rose red against a yellow sky. I got my spyglass out of my Explorer's vest and switched on the listening function. I could see the cloud rising, moving toward us and I could hear a low whooshing sound. We kept riding. And then, a huge cloud raced towards us, a rolling red wave that seemed to grow as it moved. I turned Bob away from the storm.

Kemal was doing the same thing. I could see him fighting to stay in the saddle and then I couldn't see anything at all. He was gone. I held on to my saddle horn and wrapped my scarf around my face to protect my eyes from the stinging sand. I was vaguely aware that Bob had sunk down on his knees, but suddenly all my senses were so assaulted with the raging wall of sand that I didn't know whether I was upright or not. I didn't know where Kemal was and I didn't know if I was even on Bob anymore.

The sand stung every part of me that wasn't covered, the skin above my ankles, my wrists. I tried to wrap my entire body in the scarf, but there wasn't enough of it, so I just huddled in the fetal position on the ground and I thought of Dad and of Sukey and Zander and M.K. I found myself talking out loud, apologizing to Dad for having failed.

I had the map in my head, but I had failed to find out if there was a twin city out in the desert. And now I never would.

It raged on and on and I just lay there, talking to myself and then suddenly, I thought someone else was talking, and hands were lifting me up and pushing me through the cloud of sand. White fabric filled my vision.

"Kemal?" I asked. "Is that you? Kemal?" But no one answered. I was pushed and pulled and I felt cloth over my face and suddenly the sand stopped and the noise grew quieter and there were voices, and rough hands pulled the scarf away from my face.

"Who is that?" I asked. I didn't have the energy to fight. I tried to open my eyes but they stung too much. Someone stroked my face and put warm liquid to my lips. I sipped and lay back, my body in pain. I heard voices but when I tried to open my eyes, there was only darkness.

At one point, I thought I heard Sukey's voice, telling me everything was going to be okay, and I reached out for her but found only empty space.

And then I could feel the liquid working its way into my blood, and I slept.

Fourteen

I woke up to find Kemal sleeping next to me on the floor of a small room. There was a brightly colored carpet on the ground and we were sleeping on piles of blankets, with thin sheets pulled over us. The room smelled of vanilla and cinnamon.

Not a room, I realized as I looked around, but a tent. A very large tent. The light was low but I could see the folds of fabric held up by a central tent pole. My vision was a bit blurry and I became immediately aware that my hands and feet hurt. I sat up as much as I could and heard voices in some other part of the tent. In the distance, I could see forms moving and hear the low murmur of voices speaking a language I didn't think I recognized. I immediately checked for my vest and backpack and found the familiar shapes next to me on the red carpets covering the floor. I listened to see if the sandstorm was still raging outside, but it was quiet.

"Kemal," I whispered. "Kemal. Wake up."

I reached over to shake him and he groaned before opening his eyes and staring at me with a terrified expression on his face. His eyes were bloodshot, the skin around them red and raw. I realized that mine probably looked the same and I realized why my vision was blurry.

"Where are we?" he whispered.

"I don't know. Some kind of tent."

"They must have rescued us." He took a deep breath, then shuddered. My lungs hurt every time I breathed too. When I looked down at my hands, I could see that they were raw and rashy from the sand.

Before we could say anything else, a woman dressed in long red robes came over holding a copper cup.

She held it to Kemal's lips and he took a sip.

Then she held it to mine.

"Who are you? Where are we?" I asked her.

"Shhhhhh." She put the cup to my lips again and I

drank. This time it was just cold water and one sip made me realize how thirsty I was. I had another long gulp before she helped Kemal have another drink. Then she said something in a language I didn't understand and a man came over to join her, kneeling down beside us.

"Where are we?" I asked them. I was nervous, but not afraid. There was something kind about their faces and my instincts told me they were friends, though my training told me to have one hand on my vest and backpack in case I needed to run or defend myself.

"How are you feeling?" the man asked us in English.

"Everything hurts," I told him.

"It's the sand. During a sandstorm, the wind turns little grains of sand into needles. It is terrible. It has happened to me."

Suddenly, I remembered Bob and Andrew. I sat up. "Our Dab Lizards. Did you see our Dab Lizards?"

The man looked confused. "Dabs? No. We found the two of you just outside. I heard shouting and I went out and there you were."

Kemal and I looked at each other.

"Someone guided me here," Kemal said. "Someone helped me up and brought me here."

"Me too," I said. "I remember someone in robes helping me up and then I was out of the storm. It must have been you."

"That's not possible," the man said. "We wouldn't have gone out in it." He glanced at the woman and she looked away.

"Then who brought us here?" Kemal asked. "Could it have been someone else?"

"No one can survive in the storm," the man said. "The sand does strange things to your mind. You must have imagined it."

The man's name was Gustav and his wife was Zainab. He told us that he had come to Simer City ten years ago from his home in Sweden to be a farmer. Then he had met Zainab, whose family had come to Simer City from Tyre. They had discovered they could make a good living as traders, living a nomadic life in the desert. Gustav and Zainab had a herd of more than fifty goats, and they traded milk and cheese and meat for things they needed as the traders came through on their way to Count von Rostovich's palace and the northern territories.

They had four children, twin boys who were eleven, like M.K., and two little girls, who brought us food and water and tried to speak to us in Simerian and Swedish. Kemal and I felt gradually better as the day wore on and by dinner time we felt well enough to join the family for dinner. They ate at a low table surrounded by piles of cushions, and Zainab poured sweet mint tea for everyone while Gustav sliced pieces of meat onto a platter and passed it around with bowls of olives and fruits.

We were hungry and we took more than our share of the delicious food.

"So you were taking the Dab Lizards to the palace?" Gustav asked us after we'd had a chance to eat.

"Yes." I glanced at Kemal. "Kemal's father is a Dab Lizard dealer and he asked us to bring them to trade with Count von Rostovich. Do you know him?

"Do I know him?" Gustav laughed. "I do not mingle with the likes of Count von Rostovich. He doesn't let anyone but a select few near his palace." He smiled. "It's like a fortified city. We have to trade our milk and cheese to one of his approved traders."

"And of course he takes fifteen percent," Zainab added.

"How do they get there?" I asked. "Do they have maps to the desert so they can avoid the sandstorms?"

"That's what they say." Gustav got up and cleared the food from the low table, coming back with more tea and a platter of dates and cheese. "They say that the Count built his palace near the site of a beautiful oasis, where there was once a great city that is buried in the sand."

I looked up a little too quickly and saw Kemal glance at me.

"I heard a legend about a lost city in the desert," I said, taking a chance. "A Lost City of Maps. Do you think that's where the Count built his palace?"

"There have always been legends about a lost city in the desert," Zainab told us. "When I was a girl, my mother told me stories about the Lost City of Maps." She smiled, her face illuminated by the light from the candles on the dinner table. "She had one about a handsome hero who ventured into the desert to find the Lost City of Maps. It was said that if you found it, you would be the richest man in the world, because the maps would show you where all the great treasures of the world could be found. So, my mother told me, he braved sandstorms and the attacks of dragons and the burning sun, and when he got to the city he found all the maps of the world. And he became very rich and married a beautiful princess."

All the maps of the world. Could that be what Dad wanted me to find?

"And it's supposed to be out here in the desert?" I asked her. "Maybe near the Count's palace?"

"Oh, it's just a children's story. A what-do-you-call-it? A fairy tale. If there was a lost city near the Count's palace, someone would have found it by now." She smiled, smoothing the hair of the little girl at her side.

But I wasn't so sure.

Zainab played the fiddle and after dinner she and the children entertained us until bedtime. Kemal and I were starting to feel better, but we needed a good night's sleep. And, I reminded myself, we needed another mode of transportation.

"What are we going to do?" Kemal asked me once everyone had gone to bed and we were bedded down on the carpets.

"I don't know. We could try to go on to the palace on foot. If my mileage calculations are correct, we may not be that far."

"But how would we get back to Simer City? All the food was with the lizards, remember?" I'd never heard Kemal sound quite so panicked.

"I don't know, Kemal." I was thinking about my training. A good agent takes stock of all available assets. The goats. Maybe Gustav would sell us some goats. But you couldn't ride a goat across the desert.

"We can't stay here forever," he said. "They've been so kind, but at some point we're going to have to leave."

"I know," I said. "We'll figure it out. I'm going for a walk." I was annoyed at Kemal for some reason, though I knew he was right.

Outside, the air temperature had dropped and I wrapped my scarf around my neck and face against the chilled air. The night sky was black and full of stars; they twinkled with a red glow and I tipped my head back to look at them. I walked a little ways away and then turned back to look at the tents, their silhouettes and the dark looming shadows of the mountains behind.

Something about the tents bothered me, but I couldn't figure out what it was.

So I looked up at the stars again, wondering whether Sukey was awake and looking up at them from within the walls of Simer City. Was Zander with her?

And then, because it hurt too much to think of her with Zander, I forced her out of my head and headed back to the tent.

It was the stars I dreamed about that night, stars that moved through the sky creating patterns and shapes overhead. I tried to read the shapes as though they were a secret message, but they didn't stay in place long enough to let me.

At some point in the night, I startled awake, sure someone was watching me, but when I opened my eyes in the darkness, Kemal and I were alone, his soft snoring the only sound.

Fifteen

Gustav and Zainab's youngest daughter woke us
up with the news the next morning,
"Kit, Kemal!"

She practically pulled us out the door. The sun was
bright already and I blinked a few times to make sure I
was actually seeing what I was seeing. There, milling
around outside the tent, were Bob and Andrew and the
other Dab Lizards.

"We're back in business," I told Kemal.

Gustav brought them a pail of water and some meat.
Miraculously, our rations were still on their backs and
they seemed okay after their adventure in the desert.

"Dab Lizards have very good sense of smell," Gustav told us. "That's what makes them so useful. I've always wished for a Dab Lizard. Even in the desert they are able to find prey from very far away. They must have smelled you."

"It *has* been a long time since we had a bath," Kemal laughed.

We got ready to go and thanked Gustav and Zainab and the kids for all they had done for us.

We had the lizards harnessed and ready to go when I noticed the little girls petting the smallest of the lizards, a female we'd named Lillian. Lillian was licking their faces and nuzzling them. They giggled and patted her scaly head.

"Hey, Kemal," I whispered. "Look."

"She really likes them," he said, smiling.

"What do you think? They did save our lives."

He nodded and I went over to the little girls and detached Lillian's harness from the others and handed her lead to them.

"Take good care of Lillian," I told them. "She's yours now."

Their excited shouts drew Gustav and Zainab over, and Gustav hugged me and Kemal. "Thank you, dear friends," he told us. "You will always have a home with my family."

As we moved away from Gustav and Zainab's tent, Bob started to whimper, turning around to look as the tent and the people standing around it got smaller and smaller.

"What's wrong with him?" Kemal asked.

"I don't know." But as he turned his head to look back one last time, I realized who he was searching for. "It's Lillian! Bob's in love with Lillian."

"Sorry, Bob," Kemal told him. "We gave away your girlfriend."

Bob looked sad, but he pointed his nose northwest and headed into the desert.

"Thanks, boy," I told him. "Let's try to find the count's palace."

As it turned out though, the count's guards found us first.

We'd been riding for a couple of hours when the lizards became restless. They stopped and balked and moved on only when Kemal and I kicked them gently.

Twenty minutes later, we understood why.

The landscape had changed a bit, become hillier, with giant sand dunes that obscured the horizon, so we didn't see the men until the lizards had reached the top of a high dune and we looked down to find six riders approaching from the east.

I pulled Bob up next to Andrew and asked Kemal, "What should we do? Who do you think they are?"

"I'd say they're from the palace."

I got out my spyglass and focused on the horses' riders.

They were all wearing red tunics and pants, and had what looked like swords at their waists. I remembered what Gustav had said about the count's guards. But we didn't really have any choice. We pushed the lizards on and then halted when one of the men on horseback called out to us.

"*Ostanovit!* Stop! Stop right there!"

The horses galloped towards us, sand flying around their feet.

They surrounded us, the men all talking at once. "Who are you? How did you get here?" They spoke in Russian, but when we looked confused they switched to English.

I let Kemal take the lead.

"Oh, we are coming to sell Dab Lizards to Count

von Rostovich," he stammered, making his accent much stronger than it usually was. "My father is a Dab Lizard dealer."

"Does he know you're coming?" one of them asked.

"Oh yes, I think so. At least my father said he would."

One of the guards, who had been hanging back, came up and looked at Kemal and then at me, leaning over in his saddle to study our faces. "How did you get here?"

"We, uh, we just kept riding and the, uh, the lizards seemed to know the way. They seem to be very good at finding, uh, you."

The guards glanced at each other. "Stay here," said one and they rode their stallions a couple hundred yards away and formed a little knot. They all leaned in and we could see their lips moving, but they were too far away for us to hear what they were saying. Carefully, I took out my spyglass and held it up, pretending to be studying the horizon.

"Careful," Kemal whispered. "They keep looking around and checking on us."

I carefully switched on the listening feature and turned it until I could hear them talking. They had gone back to Russian but I could understand most of what they were saying.

"… Lizards." One guard said. "The Count has been wanting to purchase more lizards."

"Yes, but with everything that is happening, he might not want anyone who is not a known trader."

"He needs those lizards," said a woman in a black helmet. "Especially if…"

"Shhh. Do not talk about that."

"They can't hear us," said another guard.

"I think we should bring them back and let them sell their lizards. The feast isn't until tonight. We can make sure they have left the palace grounds before the guests begin to arrive."

"Okay."

There was some more discussion and then the guards and their horses trotted back across the sand.

"You have how many lizards to sell?" asked the guard who seemed to be in charge, a tall blond guy with a bad sunburn on his nose.

"Ten," I told him. "We'll need these two to get back to Simer City, of course."

"They're high quality," Kemal told him. "Very healthy."

"Okay, follow us."

We set off, the guards' horses traveling a good half

mile ahead of us, the lizards loping along behind.

Dad once told me about coming upon a desert oasis when he was traveling through the Sahara. He described the strangeness of it, the way you were traveling along in the endless beige and brown of the desert and then suddenly you saw the green of palm trees.

It was almost like that, just a sudden flash of a different color and then, as we came up to the top of a bit of a rise, we saw a spreading green valley, the palm trees creating, from a distance, a sort of carpet over the sand. In the middle, we could see a small lake, fed by a river and surrounded by foliage and a spreading complex of low sand-colored houses, all leading to the huge structure sitting on a little hill overlooking the lake and surrounded by walls and geometric gardens.

"Wow," I said.

Kemal and I stared at the scene in front of us.

"I'm not… just imagining that, am I?" he asked me.

"If you are, then we're imagining the same thing."

We rode down along a wide wash and in through a heavily guarded gate in the high wall that surrounded the palace and the little village that had sprung up around it. I thought of books I'd read about the feudal system and the castles of Lords and Dukes in medieval Europe.

Every single person and animal in this settlement seemed to be there because of the count and his palace. All the foot and camel traffic went in and out of the palace gates.

The palace was massive, a beige fortification with domes and ramparts and pillars. A wide flight of stairs led up to the front doors, which seemed to be covered with gold, and I could see lush gardens spreading out behind it in every direction.

The guards took us around the side of the palace, along a path that followed the inside of the wall. As we led the Dab Lizards past the palace gardens, I could hear fountains and streams not far away and the sound of running water made me suddenly thirsty.

The palace looked new, everything shining and clean, and I couldn't see any evidence of an ancient city beneath my feet. Somehow, I'd have to explore further.

Behind the gardens and the palace, up against the high surrounding walls, was the stable.

The lizards nodded their heads nervously the way they did when they smelled something interesting and as we entered the high-ceilinged structure, I saw why. On one side of the stable were rows of camels. They were chewing and smacking their lips as they watched us walk past with the lizards.

"Hey!" Kemal shouted and I turned to find that a camel had deposited a giant clump of spit and hay on his head.

On the other side of the aisle were the more dignified-looking horses, which watched the lizards lope past with disdain. They were beautiful animals, mostly sleek black stallions, with intricately braided manes and tails.

"You can tie up your lizards there," one of the men told me when we reached a row of empty stalls at one end of the stable. "The Stable Master will want to have a look at them before we take you to the count."

We tied them up and watched as an old man wearing leather chaps and riding boots looked over the lizards. He felt their skin and checked their mouths and eyes.

"They're quite good quality," he said. "I think the count will want to see them." He nodded to the guards and one of them swung off his horse and handed the reins to one of the young boys who had appeared to tend the horses. "Your lizards will be safe while you conduct your business."

Sixteen

We told Bob and Andrew to be good and the guards led us back around the inner palace walls to the front entrance of the palace. We climbed the steps to the front door and one of the guards told us to wait there while he went in to announce us to the count. The steps were bustling with people—women holding boxes of meat and produce, merchants asking to come into the palace to present their wares.

I heard a group of boys, dressed in yellow tunics and pants, yellow scarves wrapped around their heads, tell the palace guards that they had been hired to serve at the feast.

"A feast?" I whispered to Kemal. "I wonder what's going on."

"Whatever it is, there's going to be a lot of food," he said, as we watched a long line of girls and boys carrying baskets of fruit, wine bottles, and pastries into the palace.

The guard returned and we walked through the soaring, gold-plated doors.

The interior was a mix of indoor and outdoor spaces, spacious rooms painted with murals and frescoes, tiled walls covered with beautiful and colorful designs, little courtyards with lush plants and flowers growing around tiled fountains.

We followed the guards down a hallway that branched to the left off the main part of the castle and were ushered past another group of guards, these ones armed with swords and lethal-looking pistols, and into a large office at the end of the hallway.

"Come in, come in," said a man sitting on a low couch against one wall. He had a small, brown dog sitting on his lap and the dog fixed its eyes on us as we entered the room, baring its teeth as if to warn us not to get too close. "Hello, welcome. I am Count Grigory von Rostovich. And you are?"

"I am Kemal Asker," Kemal told him. "And this is my cousin, Ian, uh, North."

I glanced over at him. *Ian North?*

Count von Rostovich was a large, bald man with very pink skin. He was wearing pink silk robes that seemed big as bed sheets, and they made him look like a large pillow. He wasn't fat exactly, just a very large person who took up a lot of space. He was drinking from a huge wine glass and every once in a while he would offer it to the dog so it could have a sip.

"Ah, the Dab Lizard traders, is that right?" One of the guards stood behind him, his hand on the sword at his waist. I had the distinct feeling that if I made any movement towards the count, I would find out exactly how sharp the sword was.

"Yes, your honor," I said. "It's an honor to be your guest, your … honor."

Kemal gave me a funny look. Perhaps I was laying it on a bit thick.

"I hear the lizards are of excellent quality. We've discovered that they make good transport in the desert and I was hoping that I might be able to buy some soon. But my guards tell me that you were under the impression you had an appointment with me. Is that right?"

Kemal stepped forward. "That's what my father told me anyway. He sent me and my cousin here to complete the transaction."

"And what is your father's name?"

"Ekrem Asker, your honor."

He stared at Kemal while he took another sip of wine. "Funny, I don't recall ever meeting him and I have an excellent memory for names. But no matter, I'm quite lucky that you happened to stop by. Now, what is your price?"

"Uh, my father said two hundred Allied dollars a lizard."

The count seemed to think about that for a moment. Then he said, "Normally, I would bargain with you. But this is a busy day and I am tired. Tell you what, one hundred and sixty each, and you've got a deal."

Kemal looked to me and I shook my head. Any Dab Lizard dealer worth his salt would negotiate the price.

"One hundred eighty," Kemal countered.

"One hundred seventy-five."

I nodded. We'd paid one hundred and eighty each for them so it would be a loss, but it was Mr. Mountmorris's money and I didn't really care. The important thing was that they'd gotten us into the palace.

Kemal smiled. "Uh, okay. Yes, your honor. That sounds like a great deal."

"I really don't have any memory of an appointment with anyone named Asker," the count said. He pushed the dog off his lap and, with great effort, stood up and walked over to the massive desk. It had lots of drawers and the sides and front were carved with ornate designs, eight-pointed stars, and floral designs.

I followed him with my eyes. The map had to be somewhere in the room. But where? I was betting it was in that desk.

"Is this your first visit out to my palace?" he asked us, watching us carefully.

"Yes," I told him. "It's really beautiful. Is the palace old? There's so much beautiful art, but it looks very well-taken care of too."

The count smiled. "It's inspired by an actual palace that belonged to a king from the Tenth century, but I finished building it only eight years ago."

"Was the king's palace on this same site?" I asked him, trying to seem only vaguely interested.

"Not far from here. It was all ruins by the time I arrived." He was watching me a bit more closely now.

"Really? Are the ruins still here?" As if he was growing suspicious too, the count's dog trotted over and sniffed at my leg.

"Are you an archaeologist?" the count asked me. "You seem very interested in ancient cities."

"No, just curious."

Kemal cleared his throat. "We should probably get going before it gets too late, uh, Ian."

The Count kept his gaze on me. "No, no, our friend here the archaeologist, he is very interested in the ruins of the old city. He turned to one of the guards. "We should give him a tour of the gardens, don't you think?" The guard didn't say anything.

I glanced at Kemal. Something about the offer felt off. A little stream of fear made its way down my spine. From the look Kemal gave me he seemed suspicious of the count's motives too.

"Uh, okay. Yes, thank you. That would be great."

The count and the guards led us out into the central part of the palace and then out into the gardens, the guards surrounding us so here was no chance of escape.

"Now, you see," the count pronounced. "My beautiful gardens!"

They were arranged around a center fountain which was covered in green tiles creating intricate patterns mirrored in the geometric designs created out of carefully trimmed hedges and plants. There was something mesmerizing about the designs. The shapes repeated endlessly, flipping and mirroring each other. One garden was an eight-pointed star, the next was its mirror image.

"It's beautiful," I told the count.

"Here you see where the gates of the old city once stood," he announced, pointing to a couple of blocks of stone sitting in the center of one of the gardens. "And over there was an archway that may have been from the king's palace. I wanted to have it in my palace."

I inspected the ruins, trying to look impressed but not too interested. Was this what Dad had wanted me to see? I tried to compare these old rocks with the map in my head. Was it possible that it matched, that the Lion Gate was over here or over there? But there wasn't enough to go on. How was I going to figure out if this was it?

When I looked up, I saw that we weren't alone in the gardens. A group of men were strolling along the paths too, a girl dressed in a long red cape following behind. She looked up at us and I met her eyes for a second before she looked away.

"I have the largest collection of palm trees outside of

Casablanca," the count told me. "And my gardens are said to be more beautiful than even the Emperor's own gardens."

"Really, the, you mean the Indorustan Emperor? Yes, of course. Well, I can believe it. These are really something," Kemal stammered.

The count turned around abruptly and strode over to us. He was so close I could smell the wine on his breath.

"I don't know who you are or what you want but I don't trust you, and if you're Dab Lizard traders from Ottomanland, then *I* am the Emperor of the Indorustan Empire. Now you've seen my gardens. Here's your money. My guards will show you to the gate and I want you to ride back to wherever you came from." He held out a hand and one of the guards dropped a heavy velvet bag into it. He handed it to me and snapped his fingers in the air. "I hope you realize that if you were five years older, you'd be dead."

He turned around and walked back into the palace, the little dog trotting along behind.

Seventeen

The guards were walking us back to the stables when they were stopped by another uniformed guard who said he had questions about the "security arrangements." They got involved in a long conversation about the palace doors and I took the opportunity to interrupt him.

"We can find our way back to our lizards," I told him innocently. "We need to get going so we can make some good progress before nightfall."

"Okay. But you must leave right away," he said. "That was our deal. I will check with the guards at the entrance gate to be sure that you left."

"Of course," I said. "I just want to get back to Simer City to spend our money anyway. Thanks!"

He scowled at us but he didn't watch us go.

Back at the stable, we saddled up Bob and Andrew and moved as many of our supplies from the herd's saddlebags into our own as we could, leaving the rest with the grateful stable boys and stable master.

I needed to get back into the palace and I was getting pretty curious about who it was that was visiting. Even during the time we'd been inside the palace, the level of activity just outside had reached a fever pitch. Women in white uniforms were carrying trays of food and flowers towards the palace and the stable boys were busy leading horses and camels in through a gate just behind the stables.

I took five Allied dollars out of the bag the count had given us and approached the stable boy who had helped with the lizards. "Hey," I whispered, holding up the coins. "If that gate is left open by accident later tonight, you can have all of this. Do you understand?"

He nodded, his eyes wide, and I smiled at him and handed him a package of dried apples from my saddlebags, which he took gratefully. Kemal and I saddled up and set off for the main gate, where we would make sure the guards saw us leave.

But first, I stopped and turned around to the look at the layout of the palace.

We had entered through the front entrance and then turned to the left to follow a long hallway to the end. A door had opened into the count's office. I followed the path we'd taken and found the outside wall of the count's office, mentally noting that the window was about five feet off the ground and that there was a large palm tree planted to the right of the window that might screen an intruder. I made a mental note of the guards' positions and their probable sightlines. And I looked again for the outlines of an ancient city, but they were hard to see. There were a few pillars that seemed to have fallen on the ground outside the walls surrounding the village, but not much else. I noted where they were and told Kemal I was ready.

The guards seemed happy to see us go.

"Thanks for everything," Kemal told them, with a big smile.

They scowled as we passed.

"See you again soon," I muttered under my breath.

We rode out into the desert until we couldn't see the palace anymore and stopped to eat. The sun had started dropping back towards the horizon and our shadows were long and ungainly looking. The lizards looked like strange, stretched-out monsters.

"Kit," Kemal asked me once we'd watered Bob and Andrew. "Did you see that girl in the gardens?"

"Yeah." I may have blushed a little. Kemal did too.

"Did she look familiar to you?"

No," I said. "At least I don't think so. She was very pretty. I think I'd remember if I'd seen her before."

"Yeah, you're right," Kemal said quickly. "I'd remember. It's just, I don't know. . . I must have been imagining it." Embarrassed, he changed the subject. "How are we going to get back without them seeing us? They were doing patrols when they found us. Won't they be doing patrols tonight too?"

"I'm betting that whoever these honored guests are, security is going to be pretty tight at the palace," I told him through a mouthful of bread and cheese. "They'll bring in everyone they've got tonight to guard the party. If we can sneak around and come in through the stable gates, I think we'll be okay. Remember that everyone's going to be at the palace for the feast."

"But won't they recognize us?"

"No," I told him. "Because we're going to be in disguise."

Eighteen

Four hours later, under cover of darkness, two boys dressed in bright yellow tunics and pants with yellow scarves wrapped around their heads, snuck up behind Count von Rostovich's stable and slipped in through the open gate.

We'd bought the robes and caps from two palace workers heading home to sleep. The yellow garments were worn by all of the count's staff and we were hoping they would help us blend in. We'd paid about four times more than the clothes were worth, but they were our best chance of disguising ourselves.

"Who are we again?" Kemal asked me.

"Local boys who were hired to help out with serving food," I told him. "I saw a bunch of them being hired when we were on the palace steps before. If anyone asks, just say you were told to clear plates and bring in platters of food. Keep your head down and hopefully those guards will be posted somewhere else. We don't need too much time, just enough to break into the count's office." *And get back to the gardens to see if I could find anything else of the ancient city.*

"Oh, is that all?"

"This is what we're meant to be doing here, Kemal, getting the maps. I don't want to be the one to tell Mr. Mountmorris we were too scared to do it, do you?"

"What if someone recognizes us?"

"Then you should run."

"Thanks a lot." But he was laughing, which I took to be a good sign.

There was a steady stream of people walking towards the palace and we joined it, the scent of blooming flowers wafting over from the gardens. As the elegantly dressed guests flowed into a large room filled with music and candlelight and sparkling crystal, Kemal and I headed for a group of girls and boys standing near the entrance and holding trays filled with glasses of a pale pink, bubbly liquid.

"Where is the kitchen?" I asked, in Simerian. "We were told to show up here to help with the serving."

They pointed to a hallway and we followed it, facing a tide of girls and boys carrying trays and serving platters in the opposite direction, and when we pushed through large swinging doors and found ourselves in a huge and busy kitchen, it was easy to each take a tray from the counters and follow the rest of the servers out into the hallway. We swept past the guests and into the huge banquet hall, and following the other servers' lead, put the plates of dates and cheese at the places on the table.

"What should we do?" Kemal whispered.

"Let's just play along for a bit," I whispered back. "When I see a chance, I'm going to try to get down to his office and search for the maps. If I'm gone more than, say, an hour, head for the stables. I'll meet you there. If you think someone's recognized you, hide and get to the stables as soon as you can."

Kemal nodded and we emptied our trays and went back for more. Once the first course was served, the guests sat down and the count came in, followed by a long line of guards dressed in fancy military uniforms and fur hats.

"They must be hot," I whispered to Kemal.

The guards—sweating profusely, I could see as they passed by—were followed by a long line of men and women dressed in all different kinds of fancy outfits— long robes, silken coats tied with a belt around their waists, lace dresses and headpieces.

"Kemal…" I whispered.

"Shhh."

One of the guards came forward and announced the guests one by one as they came up the center of the room and took their seats.

"General Yang Wei and Mrs. Dao Wei," he announced. The couple walked slowly down the center aisle, smiling and waving, and then took their seats next to the count.

"Lieutenant Chandra Chandragupta and her husband Mr. Chandragupta."

"Mr. Gregor Sikilly, division head of the Indorustan Empire's security division."

"Mr. Aristan Karimov and his daughter Anara Karimov." A tall, bespectacled man in long robes came down the aisle, followed by a girl of about our age, dressed in a blood red strapless dress and an elaborate silk headband decorated with flowers. As she passed, she turned her head to survey the room and when she came to Kemal and me, she looked startled, then met my eyes before taking her father's arm and continuing down the aisle.

"Did you just see that?" Kemal whispered. "That's the girl we saw in the gardens."

"I know and she just stared at me."

"You wish."

"Mr. Takata Itara, military advisor to the Indorustan Empire."

"Kemal," I whispered. "Kemal, do you see what—?"

The count stood up, gesturing grandly to the crowd.

"Hello! I am so pleased that everyone is here to see my beautiful oasis in the desert. As our…" He glanced over at Grego Sikilly, a small smile on his face. "…partnership begins, I wish all of my friends from the East good luck in all of their endeavors. Now please enjoy your meals." There was a hearty round of applause and everyone sat down to eat.

I grasped Kemal's arm.

"Kemal, do you see what this is?" I whispered, trying to keep my voice down. "It's an Indorustan military delegation. They must be here because they're launching an invasion."

Nineteen

"You keep serving here," I told him. "I've got to try to find those maps. The fact that they're here must mean that they have a plan in place for the invasion and they've come to get the maps. We may not have a lot of time."

I took a vase of flowers off a nearby table and held it out in front of me, walking toward the hallway to the count's office as though I knew exactly where I was going.

But there was a row of guards blocking the hallway.

"Where are you going?" one of them asked me in Russian.

"I was told to deliver these to the count's office."

"We'll deliver them," the guard said, taking the flowers from me and scowling.

"Thank you." I nodded and turned around.

I walked back to the front entrance of the palace, trying to figure out what to do. There was no way I was going to get down there from inside the palace.

I'd have to try outside.

They had lit torches in the gardens and a small group of musicians were playing small stringed instruments near the central fountain. Because everyone was eating, the gardens were empty. I walked slowly, trying to pretend I was just seeking some quiet and fresh air, while I checked out the windows on the count's office and tried to figure out how I might get in.

The palm tree I'd noticed before would provide good cover, especially now that it was dark. But the problem was that the window was covered with a metal grille and it was too far off the ground for me to try to take it off.

I needed a plan.

I took the path around the side of the palace, following the geometric designs of the gardens. The shapes were created with tall grasses, flowering shrubs and many different kinds of flowers. Stone paths wove between the gardens, repeating the shapes in the beds. I remembered reading that ancient Islamic design used squares and circles to create an infinite number of design possibilities and that the designs could contain complicated math equations and secret codes.

I searched the grounds again and found only the few bits of old stone blocks and columns. If this was the Lost City of Maps, there wasn't much left of it.

There were two guards patrolling this side of the garden and I waited until they had turned their backs and were walking down the other side of the palace to slip out of the garden and up to the palm trees near the count's office. I ducked down so the guards wouldn't see me when they turned around and came back in the other direction.

I had been right. The window was too high off the ground for me to attempt to remove the grille. But when I went around the corner I found another window, and this one, though it also had a metal grille over it, was closer to the ground. It was dark inside and when I peered through the grille, I couldn't see anyone. Everyone was at the feast. The grille had only two screws keeping it in place, one at the top and one at the bottom. I took Dad's multipurpose gadget out of my vest and used the screwdriver attachment to remove the screws. Carefully, trying not to make a sound, I lifted the grille off and hid it in amongst the palm trees in case the guards came by. The window was actually easy to open—if the Count had asked for my security advice, I would have told him not to rely on just one level of window security. But he hadn't asked me, so I slipped into his office, closed the window behind me, took off my tunic, and turned on my vest light. It was hard to know where to start. The obvious place was the count's desk, but what were the chances he'd have left it there, in easy reach of anyone he invited into the office?

No, I was betting that the map was hidden somewhere else in the office.

I decided to start with a large chest of drawers in the corner. It had six drawers, each one only two inches high—the perfect size. I opened the top drawer and was rewarded with a stack of maps.

I looked through all of them, but none seemed to show the desert around the palace. They were of faraway destinations, China and India and Mexico and other places, but not of the count's own backyard.

I checked the other drawers and was about to move on to the desk when I heard voices out in the hallway and just barely managed to squeeze into the small space between the wall and the bureau when the door opened, someone lit the candelabra hanging from the ceiling, and the count's voice boomed, "Welcome, my friends. I am so pleased that you could join me."

"And we are so pleased that you are assisting us in our important fight against the aggressions of the United States and its Allied Nations," said another voice.

I could hear the sound of everyone getting settled in chairs and then another man said, "Count von Rostovich, we appreciate your willingness to share with us the secret maps showing a viable route through the desert to Simer City. We have our air and ground forces ready for the invasion, but we must know how to avoid the sandstorms."

I pressed myself against the wall. They couldn't see me now, but if someone came around behind the desk and sat down in the chair, I'd be right in his line of sight.

I couldn't tell how many people were in the room, but from my hiding spot I counted six pairs of feet.

"Well, yes, of course you do," Count von Rostovich said. "But the question is, what is in it for me? The Allied forces, they might also be interested in these maps to cross the desert. Everyone needs to cross the desert, after all. Why should I give them to you?"

"Well, it goes without saying that we will pay your price. But of course, you must think about your loyalties here. When the Indorustan Empire wins the war, whose side do you want to be on?"

"Well," the Count said slowly, as though he were enjoying this conversation. "If I had a crystal ball and could look into the future to be sure it is you who will win this war, perhaps I might go along with your line of reasoning. But I do not know for a fact that you will be victorious, and so perhaps it would be better for me to remain neutral until this thing is decided. Wouldn't you agree, Mr. Karimov?"

"What? How dare you?" sputtered a man's voice. "Don't you know that we could crush—"

"Now, now, Daddy. We don't need to go there. At least not yet."

I couldn't see her, but I was sure it was the girl in red. *Anara Karimov.*

"But he can't just—"

"Yes he can, Daddy, because he has the map and we don't. Isn't that right Count von Rostovich?"

"Mr. Karimov, your daughter is a very intelligent young lady. I suggest you listen to what she has to say."

"What do you want?" Mr. Karimov asked.

"I want an assurance that I will be allowed to continue my, ahem, business operations, in the event of an Indorustan victory."

"I think something can be arranged," Mr. Karimov said. "Now, if you'll show us the maps."

"You didn't let me finish," the count interrupted. "I want an assurance that I can continue my business arrangements and… " He paused dramatically. "I want a million Allied dollars."

"What?" Mr. Karimov exclaimed. "How dare you? You're just a no good opportunist—"

"Daddy," the girl warned.

"That is a lot of money," said the other man. "But the Emperor has given us his full authority to negotiate. We need that map. You have your deal."

"Excellent," the count said. "Tonight, we will return to the celebration and tomorrow I will give you your route."

"Why can't we see it now?" Mr. Karimov asked.

"What is your hurry?" the Count asked. "The Allies wait for you in Simer City. They do not have maps of the desert and they cannot attack without them. Why does it make a difference when you obtain them?"

"You have to understand, Count," Mr. Karimov said.

"We fight on not one front, but on two. There are elements within our own Empire that are working against us. The sooner we can begin a conflict that will force all of our citizens to pick a side… the better."

There was a long silence and I held my breath, pressing myself into the wall. If this went on much longer, someone was going to see me.

"I have learned never to mix business with pleasure," the count said. "Tonight we celebrate, and tomorrow, you will have your map."

"Thank you," the girl said. "My father is impatient to begin. But the Emperor is deeply grateful and you will see the fruits of his gratitude once we have found victory against our enemies."

There was some shaking of hands and, from the sound of it, kissing of cheeks, and then they all filed out and someone extinguished the candles so that it was dark again. I told myself to count to one hundred once they were gone, in case the count came back for something, and I had reached ninety-seven when I heard the door of the office click softly open and I heard the barest whisper of footprints on the carpet.

I waited for the candles to be lit, but the room stayed in darkness.

Whoever it was didn't want to be seen.

I heard a soft rustle and, in the little bit of light from the gardens that filtered through the window, I looked up to find Anara Karimov behind the desk. If she looked down, she would see me. But she didn't look down. She was standing against the wall and fiddling with one of the framed pictures the count had hanging there. I hadn't seen what it was, but in the faint moonlight coming through the windows, I watched as she took it down, placed it on the desk, and removed the back of the frame.

Outside the door, I heard footsteps and voices. The count's guards, patrolling the hallway. How had she slipped back in without them seeing her?

She looked up, then went back to work, lifting a piece of paper out of the frame.

What was she doing? Was she some kind of art thief?

She held up the paper and in the moonlight coming through the window, I could see the lines drawn on the paper.

It was the map of the safe route across the Simerian Desert.

Twenty

I gauged the distance to the window, and while she was occupied with the frame, I leapt out of my hiding spot, took the map from the desk, and sprinted to the window.

She swore behind me, but very quietly. It took me a second to lift the sash and in that second, she leapt across the space herself and I felt her grab the back of my vest. But I was already propelling myself out the window and rolling onto the ground beneath and then springing back up again, ready to run. I could hear her behind me.

Clutching the map in my right hand, I ran down and into the gardens. Now I realized that I had an even bigger problem.

The guards.

All she had to do was call out to them and tell them I'd broken into the count's office.

But she didn't.

Because she had also broken into the count's office, I realized. She was as guilty as I was.

I saw the guards up ahead and I looked over my shoulder, didn't see her behind me, and slowed to a fast walk. I was in the gardens now and if I looked like I was just out for an evening stroll, I thought I could make it undetected to the other side of the palace and then back to the stable.

I was close. It had been an hour. Kemal would be waiting for me and we could escape out the opened stable gate and into the desert.

But she was one step ahead of me. I turned a corner on the path and there she was. She was leaning against a palm tree with a small smile on her face.

"That's mine."

She had been hiding behind the palm tree shading the

benches, and now she was standing in front of me on the path. The red dress looked black in the moonlight. She was holding a small knife.

"It's not yours, it's the count's. You didn't want to wait until tomorrow so you took it now. How did you know where he kept it anyway? It was a good hiding place."

She smiled and I thought again that there was something familiar about her face. "I thought there was someone hiding in the room while we were talking. You're lucky they didn't catch you. Haven't you noticed that people are nervous when they're near something they're trying to keep hidden? The count kept glancing at the wall whenever he said the word 'map' and I figured that had to be it."

"Very clever," I told her. "But I have it now."

"Mmmm. I see that." She rolled up on her toes and stretched her arms above her head then let them hang loosely at her sides. "But I know a little bit about you now and I don't think you'll get very far."

"Who are you?" How did she know anything about me? We'd only just met.

"My name is Anara Karimov. I was born in Kastannay, but now we live in Moscow. My father is a senior official with the Indorustan government. My mother is a professional cello player."

"Did your father make you steal the map?"

"Don't be ridiculous. Even with all of his impatience, he was more than ready to wait until tomorrow. But he's not as smart as he thinks he is."

"But then why... oh," I said, figuring it out. "You didn't trust the count to give you the right map. You wanted to check and see what it looked like and then you were going to put it back so he didn't know you'd seen it."

She stared at me for a moment. "You're very clever too," she said. "So you can understand why I need that back."

"Sorry." But I was stuck and she knew it. If I turned around and ran she could follow me. And the longer we stood there, the greater the chance that the guards were going to notice something was going on and come to investigate.

Just when I'd decided to turn and run for it, she sprang forward, tackling me to the ground and trying to grab the map out of my hand. I rolled over, feeling the gravel that lined the paths biting into the exposed skin at my wrists and ankles. I held the map up and out of her reach, but that allowed her to roll me again, trying to pin me down with her elbows.

There was just enough light that I could see her face clearly and it occurred to me that Kemal was right: there was something familiar about her... her eyes in particular.

I'd seen them before, and from almost this exact angle. It was only when she looked up at me and her cloak fell over her head, leaving only those wide brown eyes showing, that I recognized her.

Anara Karimov was Blue Mask!

Twenty-one

"I know you!" I had to work to keep my voice down. "You're the one who's been following me since Grygia! Why were you following me? Are you working as a spy for the Indorustans? How did you know about me?"

She didn't say anything, just kept grabbing for the map.

I rolled out from under her and leapt to my feet.

But she was fast and was up and facing me again "Please give me the map," she said. "If they find it missing, everything will be ruined."

"Sorry. I'm having trouble caring about your plan to

spy on me and help the Indorustan Empire invade Simer City." This was it. I had to get away from her. I tucked the map into my vest and took off running under the first arch and into the interior of the garden, following the running water and the sound of the central fountain.

There were four other fountains, each in the center of a garden laid out with paths creating the shape of an eight-pointed star made of two overlapping squares. In the center of each was a little shelter with benches underneath, the ceilings tiled with star-shaped patterns identical to those in the gardens.

I seemed to have lost Anara Karimov and I snuck into one of the smaller gardens and knelt down behind the fountain, hoping I'd see her run past looking for me and then could slip out and toward the stables.

I took the map from the count's office out of my vest and looked at it in the moonlight. The lines traced a route across the desert, a circuitous, winding path, switchbacking and turning back on itself but, presumably, avoiding the many paths the sandstorms took. There were numbers on the side of the map, which I suspected were dates and times that travelers should avoid crossing the desert, and I stared at the map for a long time, fixing the image in my memory.

Zander had once asked me how I memorized maps and I had tried to explain the way I stared at a section, fixed it in my mind, then closed my eyes to check my memory and moved on to the next section.

The air was warm and fragrant, with the scent of the flowers blooming all along the paths. I could hear the soothing trickle of the water in the fountains and I tipped my head back to look up at the tile design above my head.

I thought about the map of Simer City in my head, and of geometry.

And that was when I understood.

I had thought the twin city might be out here in the desert, but now I knew how wrong I'd been.

I should have stayed in Simer City.

I stood up, rolling the map again. I was tucking it into my vest when Anara Karimov came up behind me and pushed me to the ground, her knees pinning my arms, the knife at my throat. I could feel the cold metal against my skin.

"Give me the map," she said. "You really don't understand how important it is."

"Yes I do," I said. "Believe me, I do. Which is why I can't give it to you."

I knew I could probably get out from under her if she didn't have the knife.

"Okay," I said. "Put that away and I'll give it to you."

"That's charming," she said. "But I think that if I put it away, you won't be so willing to hand it over, will you? No, I'm going to to just see if I can find it." She reached down and opened my vest. Unfortunately, I'd just tucked it into an inside pocket rather than zipping it into one of the hidden compartments. She plucked it out, leapt to her feet and starting backing away, holding the knife out in front of her.

"It was nice to properly meet you," she said. "Kit. And I'm very sorry for what's about to happen."

"What do you mean?" I got to my feet, brushing gravel from my clothes and trying to figure out how I was going to get the map away from her again.

She smiled, smoothed her hair down, and tucked the map into the folds of her cloak. "I respect you, so I'm going to give you thirty seconds, but as soon as you're out of my sight, I'm going to go tell the guards that I saw you climbing out of the count's office and you're going to have the entire palace guard looking for you. Bye, Kit! I hope you—"

I had no idea what she said next because I was already running towards the palace stables.

Twenty-two

Kemal was waiting for me just outside the open stable gate, Bob and Andrew with him. He'd been leaning against the wall and staring off into the distance but when he saw me, he stood up straight and took hold of the lizards' harnesses. They swung their heads around to watch me coming.

"Kemal, we need to go now," I told him as soon as I was close enough.

"Did you get it?" He was pale in the little bit of light filtering down from the palace.

"Yes," I said. "But we really need to get out of here."

He nodded and swung into Andrew's saddle, holding Bob's reins for me until I was mounted and ready to go.

"Come on boys!" I kicked Bob's sides and he'd started to move when I heard Kemal say quietly, "Kit."

The stable boy who we'd paid to leave the gate open was standing in our way, holding a sword out in front of him. He wasn't more than ten years old and he looked terrified.

"I paid you," Kemal said to him. "You left the gate open and I paid you. That's the end of it. We need to go now."

"But the guards paid me more," the boy said, his voice shaking. "They said they'd pay me three times what you paid me if I stopped you leaving and let them know when you got back. I'm sorry, but my family needs the money."

"Kit," Kemal said in a low voice. "I'll deal with this. You start riding."

"No," I said. "I'm not leaving you here. Pay him more money."

"I'll get in trouble if I don't turn you in," the boy said. "I'm going to yell for the guards now."

I turned around to look behind us. We were fairly well-hidden from the main traffic into the castle, but there were so many guards around that someone was sure to hear him if he called for them.

"We'll pay you twice what they're paying you," I said desperately. "Just let us go."

The boy didn't say anything. He just shook his head. Behind him, we heard voices, then laughter. Two guards were approaching the stables. They hadn't seen us yet, but they would any second.

"Kit. Go!" Kemal said. "Now!"

"I'm not going to leave you. They'll put you in jail." The boy was turning towards the guards.

I cold feel Bob moving, anxious to run.

Kemal patted Andrew's neck. "No, I've got an idea. But you need to start riding."

"No, Kemal—"

"If you don't start riding, Kit, I'm going to turn myself in and tell them I tried to steal the map. This is my job. Your job is to get back to Simer City!"

I stared at him. His eyes were set in defiance, his gaze steady and grim. I knew he'd do it. "You better be right behind me," I said.

"I will. Go!"

I kicked Bob's side and hunched down in my saddle, the reins in my hand and my feet in Bob's stirrups. The desert stretched out ahead of me, dark and endless and I urged him on towards the distant horizon, towards Simer City, and Zander and M.K. and Mr. Mountmorris. And Sukey.

I rode until I couldn't stay awake anymore. He'd had a good meal and a rest at the count's stables and Bob could have kept going all night, but after I fell asleep and almost fell out of the saddle, I pulled him up and stopped for a rest. With the moon high overhead and the air cooling fast, I wrapped myself up in my scarf and curled up against Bob for a nap. I needed to get some sleep and get my head straight for the rest of the journey.

When I woke up, it was still completely dark, no sign of the sun over the far horizon. Now that I'd had a little sleep, I started to feel guilty about leaving Kemal. What kind of a friend was I? If the guards had caught him, he was in big trouble and it would be a long time before anyone would be able to help him, if ever.

And I didn't even know if it had been worth it.

I knew that there was a safe route across the desert and I could give it to Mr. Mountmorris, but I also knew there wasn't enough time for our military to get to the border before the Indorustan army got to Simer City.

And somewhere there was another map, a map Dad wanted me to find. But I needed time to look for it and if there was about to be an invasion, time was exactly what I wouldn't have.

I felt very alone all of a sudden and even Bob's gentle snoring and the solid feeling of him beneath my head didn't take away my sense of being completely and totally on my own.

Suddenly, Bob's head snapped up and he jumped to his feet, knocking me to the side.

"What is it, boy?" I whispered.

He made one of his little hooting sounds and cocked his head, listening to the night air. I got up, brushing sand off my clothes, and got into the saddle. Someone was coming. I waited, not sure which direction to go, but after a few minutes, he relaxed again. I was getting ready to dismount again when I heard the sound of another lizard hooting and in the moonlight I could see Andrew racing towards us, Kemal on his back.

The sun rose in the distance as Kemal told me what had happened at the palace. Kemal had stalled the boy at the stable until I was out of sight and then he'd said that if he told the guards we were still on the palace grounds, Kemal would tell them that the boy had left the gate open for us. For a minute, Kemal thought he'd convinced him, but suddenly the boy had seemed to be overcome with fear and he'd started shouting for the guards.

"I didn't know what to do," Kemal told me. "If I started riding, I'd lead them toward you. But if I tried to escape and hide somewhere in the palace, I knew they'd eventually find me. I thought I might lead them off into the desert, but in another direction, but then I worried about getting lost. I didn't know what to do, Kit. But then I looked up and that girl was watching us. The boy was about to say something to the guards when she started yelling about a boy hiding in the count's office or something and all the guards ran to her and she took them in the direction of the palace. I didn't wait around. I told Andrew to find Bob, as fast as he could. And here we are!"

"I'm really glad to see you," I told him. "Thank you for staying behind. If something had happened, I don't think I could ever have forgiven myself."

"Kit, I told you. My job is to make sure you can do your job. Now what happened to you? Did you get the map?"

I told Kemal about everything that had happened, about the count's meeting and Anara Karimov.

"So Anara was Blue Mask?" Kemal looked like he still couldn't quite believe it. "And she has the map. Which means that the Indorustans have it, but we don't."

"Yeah." I took a bite of the slice of bread that Kemal handed me. While I'd been fighting with Anara Karimov, he'd refilled the saddle bags with food and water for the trip back to Simer City.

"What are you going to tell Mr. Mountmorris? Wait, why are you smiling, Kit?"

I swallowed the bread and said, "Because before she took it from me, I memorized it."

"You're serious?"

I nodded and Kemal cheered. "So you carried out the mission? You did what you were supposed to do? Now we have the route across the desert. We can get back that way and we won't have to worry about the sandstorms."

"We don't have time," I told him. "The route avoids the sandstorms by winding and backtracking all over the place and avoiding traveling at certain times. It would take us too long. The Indorustans have tanks and who knows what else. They'll be able to cover the same ground much more quickly. Simer City won't know what's coming. We'll have to just risk it."

He studied me for a long moment and then he said,

"Okay. You're the boss." But there was something in his eyes I couldn't quite read.

"You okay?" I asked him.

He hesitated, then asked, "Kit, is there anything else you want to tell me?"

I looked up at him. What did he know? I had been so careful not to let on that I had another reason to be here in Simeria, a reason besides the job Mr. Mountmorris had asked me to do.

"No, why?"

He hesitated and I had the feeling he'd been about to say something. But instead he just shrugged and said, "We better get going."

I felt guilty all of a sudden. Kemal had risked his life to help me and here I was lying to him about why. But I couldn't tell him that so I just said, "Thank you, Kemal. I'm glad it was you Mr. Mountmorris sent to watch out for me."

It was a long day of riding, the air hot and dry, the sun relentless overhead, and I was anxious thinking of what I'd discovered about the Lost City of Maps while in the count's gardens. I needed to get back to see if I was right, and I needed to get back to warn the city. But there was no shortcut, nothing but the slow, hot slog across the endless desert.

On the second day, we were heading southwest as the sun sank in the sky when the lizards started to get anxious.

"What do you think it is?"

"I don't know," Kemal said. "Traders?"

Bob and Andrew seemed really excited now, turning their heads from side to side and wagging their tails back and forth.

"They don't seem nervous, the way they did before," I said. "They seem almost—"

"Excited," Kemal finished. "You don't think…?"

But before he could finish, the lizards sprinted over the top of a sand dune. A white tent appeared against all the beige and then Bob and Andrew were running towards Gustav and Zainab's tent and, of course, Lillian the lizard.

Twenty-three

"We're so happy and relieved to see that you are okay," Gustav told us over supper that night.

"Lillian is happy too," said their youngest daughter. From outside the tent, we could hear the lizards' delighted chirps and clucks as they reacquainted themselves with Lillian.

"Did you make it to the count's palace? What was it like?" Zainab asked.

Kemal and I glanced at each other. I wasn't sure how much to tell them, so we just said that we'd made it and that it was as beautiful and opulent as everyone had described.

"You should come back to Simer City with us," I told them. "It's not going to be safe out here once the invasion starts. They'll probably evacuate the city and you can go too. We know now that they'll be bringing tanks and troops, maybe giant flying machines with guns on them. You're right in their path."

But Gustav didn't seem worried. He said he thought they would be fine and that they'd be safer out here than in the city.

"Gustav, I don't think you understand," Kemal said. "The Indorustans won't let Simerians stay out in the desert. They may destroy your tents, they may put you in prison."

Gustav and Zainab exchanged a glance and Gustav shrugged and said, "We can take care of ourselves. You don't need to worry."

I went outside to check on the lizards. The desert air was cooling and I could smell smoke from the cooking fire and the chocolatey scent of the cake we'd just eaten. I stood for a moment and looked up at the sky. Something was bothering me. It was the way Gustav had looked at Zainab when he'd said he wasn't worried. Why wasn't he worried? The only explanation was that he didn't think the Indorustans could hurt them.

I leaned against one of the tent poles and looked up again, at all the stars and planets. At the moon. The desert was so quiet and I realized how much I'd been counting on Marek to show up somewhere along this journey. But he hadn't. Not even once. He'd left me all alone.

Or maybe he had tried but he'd gotten lost in sandstorm like all the poor souls who like us hadn't been lucky enough to be saved by... whoever it was who'd saved us, who'd gotten us out of the storm and—

Wait a minute. I looked down at the sand, at the tent pole buried in the ground, at the bottom edge of the tent buried about an inch in the sand. And then I thought of Dad's map and the gardens at the count's palace.

"Gustav," I said breathlessly, rushing into the tent and sitting down on the carpet next to him. "Gustav, you said that you opened the tent and Kemal and I were out there in the sandstorm. But that's not what happened is it? It was you who saved our lives, wasn't it?"

Kemal was looking from Gustav to me and back again.

"But that's not possible," Kemal said. "We were miles from here. You said so yourself."

"We *were* miles from here. And Gustav and Zainab found us and brought us here. They saved our lives."

Gustav didn't say anything. He glanced at Zainab, who looked guilty.

"Think about it Kemal. When I went outside after the sandstorm, after we were feeling better, something bothered me about the tent. I just realized what it was. I could see the spot where the poles went into the ground. If that tent had been up before the sandstorm, it would have been half buried. But it wasn't." I looked at Gustav. "Which means you rode out the storm somewhere and *then* put up the tent."

"But …" Kemal looked confused. "How is that possible? There's nothing out here. Where could they have gone?"

I sat down and started talking. "The story goes that only the count had maps showing the safe route through the desert. He told a few trusted traders about them and those traders protected the routes with their lives—or the count's guards did it for them.

"But something about that didn't make sense to me. There have always been travelers in the desert, families like yours who live out here and get around, and the sandstorms would make it almost impossible to live out here. So I think there's another way of getting through the desert to Simer City and I think that it's where you took us when you found us in the sandstorm. You hid out there and then when it was over, you set up the tent and you took care of us. You gave us something to drink so that we wouldn't wake up before the storm was over."

"What?" Kemal was looking at me incredulously. Gustav and Zainab didn't say anything. "What's the route? What are you talking about Kit?"

"The garden at the count's palace got me thinking… about a lot of things. But one of them was the idea of underground water sources in the desert. I think there are complexes of underground caverns, passages, that people use to get across the desert while avoiding the sandstorms. Isn't that right, Gustav?"

What I didn't say was that I was pretty sure there was more than just caverns under Simer City.

Gustav stood up and started clearing the plates from the table. He put them into a large basket and started wiping them down with a damp cloth.

"Gustav?" I said again. "We need to get to Simer City. If we can't warn the people there, there won't be time for them to escape. They'll need to hide. Please."

It took him a long moment, but finally he and Zainab exchanged a long glance and she spoke.

"It was just a story in my family, about the tunnels under the desert that let you avoid the sandstorms when they came. As I got older, my uncle told me about them. He said only a few people knew about them, but that there were traders who got across the desert through the tunnels. Others learned how to avoid the sandstorms."

"Can you show us?" Kemal asked her. She looked down, avoiding his eyes.

"I wouldn't ask if it wasn't important, Zainab," I said. "Can you take us?"

She nodded to Gustav.

"In the morning," he said. "In the morning I'll take you."

He woke us early the next morning and we all looked on while Bob and Andrew said goodbye to Lillian. Then we thanked Zainab and the kids.

Gustav dressed in a long cloak and packed a cloth rucksack with food and embraced Zainab and the children. "I'll be back soon," he said. "You know what to do. If you think you are in danger, go to the tunnels. I'll meet you there."

We followed Gustav out into the desert for a mile or

so. Suddenly he stopped, pushed a rock aside with his foot, and bent down to brush the sand away from a metal ring attached to what looked like a piece of wood. He lifted it and we saw a sloped ramp leading down into the ground.

"Okay," he said. "I will lead you and the lizards part of the way, just until the next entry point. But I have to warn you. The tunnels can be dangerous. Sometimes traders wait for people to come through and they rob them."

"I don't think Bob and Andrew will let anything happen to us," I said.

"But people may want to try to steal them," Gustav said. "You must be very careful."

He descended the wooden ramp and we followed, coaxing the lizards along, until we found ourselves in a dark tunnel, just big enough for the lizards. There was something creepy about moving forward in almost total darkness, not knowing what was ahead, but Gustav reassured us every once in a while and soon we got used to just giving up control to the lizards and letting them lead.

At first, Bob and Andrew balked, making nervous little clucking noises and stopping suddenly. But eventually, they got used to the feeling of the tunnel and Gustav told us that

Dab Lizards were actually good at traveling underground; they were used to hunting at night and they liked darkness.

"These tunnels have been here for many, many years. We don't know who built them. They go all the way to Simer City."

"Does the count know about them?" Kemal asked. "It seems incredible that the secret could have been kept all these years."

"The count doesn't know about them. He has the maps of the desert and he can get across that way." Gustav smiled. "But we will beat him every time."

"Gustav, have you ever heard of anything other than tunnels down here?"

It was a risk, but I might not have much time once I got back to Simer City and I needed to do whatever I could to figure out why Dad had wanted me to follow the map. I thought I knew, but it was going to be hard to do what I needed to do when I got there.

"What do you mean?"

"I mean do you think there could be rooms, or larger, uh areas? Anything like that?"

"Not that I've heard of," Gustav said. "There are a lot of tunnels though."

We rode on for almost an hour, Gustav moving

quickly ahead of us, and then we heard him say, "This is where I leave you, my friends." We heard hinges squeak and then there was a sudden burst of light and he was standing on another ramp leading up to the desert.

"Good luck," he said. "You will come to a fork in about an hour. Hang to the left and you will travel for another hour or so before you will come to another fork. Take the left fork and it will end in a door like this one. It brings you out into a small square behind a shop next to the Snake Gate."

"We'll need to get to the military base," I told him. "How do we get there?"

"You won't be far," he told me. "It's about a mile north of where you'll come out."

"Thank you, Gustav," I told him. "We may be able to get people evacuated because of you. Will your family stay in the tunnels once the invasion starts?"

"Yes," he said. "Zainab is already packing our things. We can stay down there as long as we need to. Goodbye, my friends and good luck."

He waved and closed the door and then we were alone in the tunnel again.

Twenty-four

We followed Gustav's directions and came out into the light a couple of hours later. As he'd told us, the entrance to the tunnels was in a small square behind a shop near the Snake Gate and we checked to make sure no one was watching before we led the lizards out into the open.

The city was quiet in the noonday heat. Knowing what we knew, the calm seemed eerie and I wanted to shout to people to get inside, to hide, to tell them that they should pack up and leave the city.

"They have no idea," Kemal said quietly, watching a

boy play with a puppy next to the road. "They have no idea what's coming."

"Do you think there's enough time to evacuate the city?"

"I don't know. It depends on whether there are enough vehicles, whether they can run more trains to get everyone out. I just don't know, Kit. It might be safer for people to stay in their houses once it starts."

We rode north on the lizards, keeping the sunset to our right, and pretty soon the rough cobblestoned streets gave way to paved ones and we saw a complex of sand-colored buildings with a fence around it that had to be the base.

I was about to tell Kemal that we needed to be careful when I heard a loud squawk and looked up to find a familiar black silhouette against the blue sky.

"Pucci!" I shouted, and he came flapping down on to my shoulder. Bob turned to see what this strange creature was and Pucci gave him a condescending glare before nuzzling into my neck murmuring, "*Kit back. Kit back.*"

"Pucci," I said. "Where's Zander?" He bobbed his head and then took off, flapping up and over the outside wall of the base and disappearing into the complex of buildings.

We tied Bob and Andrew up at the gate, hoping they wouldn't scare anyone, and sat down on a low wall to wait.

"Do you think he'll come?" Kemal asked me.

"If he's here. He might be off on a training mission or something."

"But wouldn't Pucci be with him?"

He was right. I was just about to tell him so when I heard Pucci call and when I turned around, I saw Zander running towards me.

He didn't slow down, and the hug nearly knocked me over, but I was so happy to see him that I didn't care.

"You're okay!" he shouted. "You're really okay." He hugged Kemal too, and then he spotted the lizards. Bob made his funny hooting noise and I waved a hand at him to let him know everything was okay.

"Are those your, uh, lizards?" he asked.

"Yes, but I don't have time to explain now. Zander, the Indorustans are in the desert. They're going to invade Simeria and we need to start getting people out of the city. We may not have a lot of time."

His eyes widened. "How do you know?"

"Zander, you just have to trust me. It would take too long to explain. They need to start making a plan for getting people out of the city. I'm going to have to talk to Mountmorris, but I don't think he and Foley will do what needs to be done to get people out. I have a route across the desert that our troops can take, so they can try to stop the invasion. But I need you to think about an evacuation."

He stared at me for a long moment and I could tell that he was deciding whether or not he should believe me. He reminded me very much of Dad in that moment, his blue eyes intent, his mind churning through plans and possibilities.

Finally, he nodded and started walking towards the gate and the main building. Kemal and I followed him up the steps.

"I'm going to go and see if I can find Joyce and a few officers who I trust," he told us. "I'll tell someone to send Mr. Mountmorris to you. Are you sure about this?"

"I'm sure." I had gone over and over it while we were in the tunnel. I had to give Mr. Mountmorris the route. It was the only way to stop the invasion before it reached the city.

"He might keep you here. He might send you back. You know that, right?"

He might lock you up so that you can't go find the Lost City of Maps.

"I have a plan. I don't know if it will work, but I have to take the chance."

"Okay. He'll be here soon. Once I tell them, it's all going to happen pretty fast." He hugged me again. "Be careful, Kit."

"You too. Tell M.K. and Sukey that I'm okay?"

He nodded and disappeared down a hallway. Kemal and I waited in silence for five minutes before three young soldiers came running down a different hallway and told us to put our hands up. We did as they said and they roughly led us down the hallway and pushed us into a small room.

"Stay here," one of the soldiers said.

"As if we had any choice," I said, as we heard the sounds of them bolting the door on the outside.

"What are they going to do to us?" Kemal whispered.

"Hopefully nothing," I said. "After all, we both did what we were supposed to do. I can tell them how to get across the desert. But…"

"But what?"

"I can't help feeling like it's a trap somehow."

"What kind of a trap?"

"I don't know. That's what bothers me. We don't have any choice though. Hopefully Zander can figure something out."

"Kit," Kemal said. "If you want me to—"

He stopped talking as the door opened and Leo Nackley and Mr. Mountmorris walked in. Leo Nackley was dressed in desert camouflage and Mr. Mountmorris had on a flowing beige tunic and loose beige pants. His hair looked different than I remembered and it took me a minute to realize that he'd dyed it pink. The long wispy strands looked like cotton candy clinging to his skull.

"Hello, Mr. West," Leo Nackley said. "What a surprise to see you here. We had heard you'd been, uh, expelled from Grygia. And yet here you are."

Francis Foley entered the room behind them and I felt his chilly gaze on me. He was wearing desert camouflage fatigues, just like Leo Nackley's, but his were stiff and starched. I could sense Kemal's nervousness as he fidgeted next to me.

"Well, here I am!" I said in what I hoped was a cheery voice.

Leo Nackley scowled and I saw his right hand curl into a fist at his side.

It was Mr. Mountmorris who saved me from whatever was going to happen next. He leapt forward, shouting "Mr. West! You're back, I see! You survived the desert!"

His eyes were shining behind his glasses and the little lights embedded in his ears shone bright pink to match his hair. I could see the hope and nervousness and excitement on his face.

"Do you by any chance have something for me?"

Twenty-five

"What are you talking about?" Leo Nackley asked Mr. Mountmorris. "What does he have?"

"I'll let Mr. West show you," Mr. Mountmorris said. "Where is it?" He had a greedy look in his eyes that had started to be familiar to me.

But I was holding all the cards. I stood up and pretended to check the pockets of my pants, then put my hands out at my sides. "Oooops," I said. "Looks like I don't have it on me."

"What is going on here?" Leo Nackley shouted. He was furious, his face red, his eyes small and angry, looking from me to Mr. Mountmorris and back again.

"Luckily for you, I have it up here," I said casually, pointing to my forehead. "If you'll bring me a piece of paper and a pencil, I can make you a copy."

The paper came very quickly and I enjoyed taking my time drawing out the map of the route across the desert that I had memorized in the gardens of the count's palace. I put the dates and times when the sandstorms were likely to hit at the bottom of the paper. When I was finished, I turned it over and stood up, going to the window and looking out at the base's training yard.

Mr. Mountmorris snatched it off the table and handed it to Foley, who sat down at the table at the other end of the room and studied it carefully.

"I saw the original of this map in the palace of Count Grigory von Rostovich, in the Northern Simerian desert," I told them. "It shows a safe route through the desert, a route that would allow our forces to avoid the deadly sandstorms that plague the area and to launch a full-scale defense of the Indorustan invasion of Simeria" I glanced at Kemal and added. "It was only through the assistance of Kemal Asker that I was able to get the map and then get out safely. Unfortunately, the actual map was taken from me by an Indorustan operative, but I was able to memorize it."

"Sounds very dramatic," Mr. Mountmorris said, his eyes wide.

Leo Nackley's scowl had grown bigger and bigger as I spoke and he looked like he was about to explode with anger. But I kept going.

"While I was at the palace, I was able to discover that an Indorustan delegation was visiting and that the Empire has plans to invade Simeria in the next couple of days by launching an attack on Simer City. It may be tomorrow. It may be today. We need to evacuate the city."

"What the…?" Leo Nackley was on his feet already. "How in God's name did you get that? How did you..?" He turned to Mr. Mountmorris. "Did you know about this? Did you send him on this… *mission?*"

Mr. Mountmorris gave him a reassuring pat on the shoulder.

"Leo, calm down. I asked Mr. West to see if he could get this map for us. You know how difficult it's been to get an adult, uh, employee, into the desert. It seems my instinct was correct. Now, gentlemen, I think you would agree that it doesn't make any sense to waste time interrogating Mr. West."

Francis Foley was watching me with the small gray eyes that had always reminded me of a shark's.

"Thank you, Mr. West," he said. "We have been trying to acquire this map for many years."

"How can you just…?" Leo Nackley was really angry now.

"Leo, I want you to meet with the trainee officers and make sure our plan is being implemented. I'm sure you can understand that Mr. Foley and I have some important conversations and meetings ahead of us in order to plan for the military operation. Mr. West, I ask that you stay here on base and wait for instructions."

"But—" I protested. I needed to get over to the old city and I needed to do it now.

Mr. Mountmorris fixed his eyes on me, staring long enough that I felt uncomfortable. "I'd ask you to obey orders, Mr. West."

And then he and Francis Foley were gone. Leo Nackley followed them, complaining about me and about Mr. Mountmorris's terrible judgment.

Kemal and I were kept in the room for almost three hours, as military officials debriefed us. They wanted to know everything about the count's palace, about the sandstorms and how many guards he had and who the Indorustan officials had been. They brought us food and water, but all I wanted was to get back to the old city. I thought I might have figured out the secret of the Lost City of Maps, but what I hadn't figured out yet was why Dad wanted me to go there.

When they had finished with us, they brought us up to another room on the third floor of the Military Intelligence building, locked the door from the outside and left us alone.

"What now?" Kemal asked.

"Now we figure out how to get out of here," I told him. The room had one window, which looked out across a small parking area filled with SteamCycles and Steam-Jeeps. I tried the window, but like the door, it was locked from the outside and I couldn't see how to access the lock.

Kemal tried the door, rattling the doorknob and slamming his shoulder against the door, but while the building itself looked like it had been hastily constructed with whatever materials they'd been able to find, someone had put some thought into the security of this room.

I looked out across the yard. If only we could get someone's attention, maybe they could go get Zander and he could get us out. But I knew what a long shot that was. Chances were that if we got someone's attention, it would be a guard's.

But then I saw something that made me grab Kemal's arm and say, "Look!"

On the exterior wall of the building next to us, a small girl was methodically climbing towards the roof. She had a length of rope slung around her upper body and she was using the windows and the tops of the concrete blocks in the wall to climb up the outside of the building.

"Is that… is that M.K.?" Kemal asked.

"No, it can't be. How would she…?" But we watched as she continued to climb and when she got within one hundred yards of our window, I recognized her blond hair and Explorer's vest. I knocked on the glass to try to get her attention. She didn't look up though, and pretty soon she disappeared over the top of the roof.

"What is she up to?" I said, almost to myself.

"Do you think she even knows we're here?" Kemal asked.

"I don't know."

Kemal and I watched the yard but it was still empty, and we both jumped back when something slapped the window and then, a few seconds later, we heard a loud curse word and M.K., hanging onto a rope, slammed against the glass. She used her feet to bounce off the wall and then waved cheerfully at us before she stopped swinging and took a screwdriver out of her vest pocket and started working on the window lock.

It only took her a couple of minutes, and when she gestured for us to open it, Kemal and I lifted the sash and pulled her in.

I hugged her tightly and didn't let go until she said, "We have to get out of here," and whistled twice. In response, two ropes came hurtling down off the roof and we climbed out onto the window sill.

"Hey, Yoren," said a familiar voice.

I felt my stomach seize up. I looked up to find Sukey's face peeking down at us from the roof and it was all I could do to say, "Hey, Ludmilla. How's the family?"

She laughed. "It's good to see you. Hey, Kemal. Now let's get out of here before anyone spots you."

Kemal and I rappelled down the side of the building on the ropes, Sukey and M.K. right behind us. When we reached the ground, Sukey hugged me and then Kemal.

"Are you really okay?" she asked me, her smile reaching every corner of her face.

"I'm fine. How did you know where we were?"

"We heard Mr. Mountmorris telling the soldiers to take you up there. M.K. and I stole the ropes from the mechanic's shop."

"Well, thanks for rescuing us."

"You're welcome."

She smiled again, but there was something underneath it that told me she was really nervous, maybe even scared. Her normally alive eyes were still and watchful, the lights in her ears unblinking, a solid dark green.

Suddenly, a loud siren sounded.

It echoed once, twice, three times across the desert and off the buildings, filling the air. Almost immediately, we sensed a change on the base, a hurrying and bustling. People started to come out of the buildings and pour into the sheds in the yard. We heard engines spring to life and shouted instructions coming from all directions.

"That's it," Sukey said. "That's what we've been training for. I've got an hour to report to the air base." She smiled and I could see that the fear had come to the surface, but there was something else there too, something excited and proud. "My first solo mission."

It was so good to see them that I'd forgotten for a moment that I needed to get back to the old city. "Sukey, M.K., I have to get back to the old part of the city. It's important," I told them. "Kemal and I left our Dab Lizards out front, but I'm sure they've moved them by now. I think I'll have to walk."

M.K. and Sukey exchanged a look and then M.K. nodded.

"Go that way," she said, pointing to a path leading between two buildings. She pulled two broad-brimmed desert camouflage hats out of her pocket and gave them to us. "Put those on and meet me around front. We'll get you there."

The base was on high alert now. People in uniforms had filled the yards and training grounds and we could hear more sirens and steam engines starting outside. Sukey led us between the buildings and we kept close to the walls, trying to blend in with the trainees and soldiers reporting for duty. But I was worried that any minute now, someone was going to notice Kemal and I were gone.

"This way," Sukey said, pointing to another path. "We're almost there."

We came out at the main entrance to the base and found a place to stand where we hoped we wouldn't be too noticeable.

"Don't you have to go back and report for your mission?" Kemal asked Sukey.

"I've got…" She checked her chronometer. "Forty minutes. It's okay. I want to make sure you get out of here safely." SteamJeeps had started leaving the base in single file and Kemal and I turned away from the road in case anyone we knew was on them.

"Uh oh," Sukey said after a few minutes. "I think they've realized you're gone."

I looked up and saw a line of soldiers, led by Leo Nackley, running out of the main gate, looking around and pointing towards the road.

"Don't move too fast," Sukey whispered. "But you should probably start running now."

"How are we supposed to run without moving fast?" Kemal whispered back.

"Just do it!" Sukey grabbed my arm and we started sprinting away from the base back toward the city.

"There they are!" someone shouted. I didn't turn around to look, but I knew there were a lot of soldiers and I knew they were probably pretty fast runners.

"They saw us. We've got to lose them," I told Kemal and Sukey. "Sukey, you head back. I don't want you to get in trouble."

"I'll be fine. Just run."

We did.

As soon as we could, we got off the main road from the base into the city.

Twenty-six

We'd been running for ten or fifteen minutes and I didn't know how much longer I could keep going at this pace when we heard voices behind us shouting, "They went down there!" and then Leo Nackley shouting, "Get them!"

"Find somewhere to hide!" I told Kemal and Sukey. Sukey was behind me, Kemal in front and we followed him into a little alleyway between two shops and out onto a parallel street leading to the city gates.

But the soldiers saw where we'd gone and we heard their voices behind us as we ran. They were going to catch us, I realized. They were going to catch us and my escape from Grygia, the trip across the desert, taking the map from Anara, everything—it would all be for nothing.

A Steam engine chugged behind us. They had us. This was it. There was nowhere for us to go. I turned around to surrender.

"Get in! Quick. They're right behind us."

It was M.K.

Driving a SteamJeep.

Kemal and Sukey and I jumped into the back and M.K. slammed her foot down on the accelerator, squealing along the street toward Simer City.

Once we were sure we'd lost Leo Nackley and the soldiers, we rode along silently, the Jeep bumping over the rutted roads. In the new part of the city, no one seemed to have any idea about what was going on. People were going about their business, shopping, and strolling the streets. Children played with a large leather ball in a square and old men drank tea at the outdoor cafe where I'd had lunch the day I first arrived in Simer City.

"Okay," Sukey said. "Do you know what's going on?"

"The Indorustans are going to invade," I told her. "You need to get back to base—if they don't arrest you—and someone needs to evacuate the city. I told

Zander and he said he'd see what he could do, but I'm worried he won't have time."

"I'll be fine," Sukey said. "Let's get you where you need to go and then we'll make sure Zander doesn't need any help evacuating the city. Then I'll head back. And don't worry. They're not going to arrest me. They need me too much."

"Where do you want me to take you?" M.K. asked me.

"The Leopard's Gate. It's important. I can't tell you why, but it is."

Sukey met my eyes and I nodded to let her know it was related to Dad's map.

M.K. pulled up in front of the gate. I turned to look at them. "Be careful. Kemal and I gave them a safe route across the desert, but there are terrible sandstorms and the Indorustans have flying machines and tanks, just like we do. And they've been planning a lot longer. Just—be careful, okay, Sukey?"

She reached for me and hugged me for a long moment. "I will. You too. Okay?"

I nodded. Then I hugged M.K. and told her to be careful too and finally I hugged Kemal and told him I'd see him soon.

"You sure you don't want me to come with you?"

"I'm sure," I told him.

They got back into the Jeep.

I didn't watch them go.

I didn't have time.

Twenty-seven

The Leopard's Gate loomed above me.

This was it. This was why I was here.

When I'd arrived in Simer City, I'd been confused to find the Leopard's Gate where I'd expected the Lion's Gate to be, and vice versa.

After hearing about the Lost City of Maps, I had wondered if there was another city with the same layout but with the gates reversed, the Lion's Gate at the northern entrance, the Leopard's Gate at the south.

But then, standing in the gardens at the count's palace, I had recognized the design of Simer City as a repeating geometric design. The streets were overlapping squares, the four gates were the edges of the squares that could be repeated endlessly, or mirrored in another design.

I'd looked up at the sky and thought about the stars. The stars were like a map for travelers, for lonely people all over the world, dreaming of others looking at the those same stars. But they were a map you *looked up at*, and hiding in the garden I'd held the stolen map above my head and imagined homesick people, hiding in a secret city, looking *up* at the map rather than down at it.

That was when I'd realized that there must be another city, closer than I had imagined, a city beneath Simer City, identical in almost every respect.

The streets were empty now at the hottest part of the day and I was able to look around the Leopard's Gate without attracting too much attention. The central archway was exactly the same as the Lion's Gate, but the leopard's head looked out from the top, rather than the lion's. The head was huge and intricately carved, so that even all these years later, after time and sand had worn the surface of it away, the leopard looked out with a sparkle of intelligence in its eyes, and the surface of its coat almost looked like it might feel sleek and smooth to the touch.

All down the sides of the archway were more carvings—of a running leopard and a sitting one, of a leopard with three baby leopards. I ran my fingers over the carvings, pushing on them and looking for hidden levers or buttons.

There was nothing.

The city walls stretched out on either side of the Leopard Gate and I walked along each side for one hundred yards or so, looking for anything that seemed out of the ordinary. The stone walls were pockmarked with age, but none of the blocks seemed to have been moved. I checked again. I was stumped.

I wandered around looking at the small shops and houses nearby, searching the surface of the stone walls for anything unusual.

It was only when I returned to the Leopard Gate that I noticed what I hadn't noticed before. Amongst the carved leopards on the wall to the right of the archway was one that looked slightly different.

Was I imagining it?

As I looked more closely, I saw that it wasn't a leopard, but a lioness, the shape of her head and body just slightly different from those of the leopards.

Excited now, I pushed on the carved head of lioness and felt it depress just a little bit.

Okay, I wasn't imagining that. I checked to make sure no one was watching and looked for some sort of opening, a door or entrance that had been unlocked by the mechanism behind the lioness.

I checked all around the gate, inside and out, and all along the wall on either side.

Nothing.

I stood there thinking. The lioness had been hidden amongst the leopards. Maybe there was a leopard hidden among the lions too.

I started running.

The residents of Simer City were just starting to come out of their houses now that the sun had started its daily descent towards the horizon, and as I ran toward the Lion's Gate, I had to dodge people heading out to the market or the cafés. I wanted to yell at them to get inside, to get out of the city, but I knew that would cause panic and I needed to get to the Lion's Gate to see if my theory was correct.

This time I knew what I was looking for. I found it after only a few minutes of looking: a leopard, hidden amongst the carved lions on the lion's gate. I pressed on it, feeling it engage some kind of mechanism behind the stone.

An old woman carrying a basket walked through

the gate and I waited until she was out of sight before I inspected the interior walls of the Lion's Gate.

The huge blocks of stone were all in place. No doors or staircases, no openings.

What was I missing? It had seemed like such a perfect solution to the mystery of the map. I needed to find both the lion and the leopard in order to open the secret door. I had found them, but there was no door at the Lion's Gate, which had been the traditional entrance to the city.

But not when you flipped the map.

When you flipped the map, when you imagined looking up at it from below, the Leopard's Gate *was* the Lion's Gate.

I took off then, running back towards the Leopard Gate, hoping against hope that no one had found the entrance while I'd been gone. It took me another ten minutes and I felt the whole energy of the city shift in that time.

People knew. People knew something was happening. *Please. Please. Please.*

A siren sounded somewhere close by. Then another one.

The streets were full of people now, everyone out and filling the streets. A few military vehicles appeared,

SteamTrucks filled with soldiers carrying large guns, heading towards the east and the desert, SteamJeeps rattling along the cobblestone streets. I kept my head down and kept walking.

I was almost to the Snake Gate when a huge *whoosh* filled the air, and just as I registered a long, high whining sound in the sky above me, there was a deafening boom.

Then another one.

I looked up to find a huge flying machine overhead. From the territories, north of the city, I could see smoke rising above the city.

The Indorustans were here.

too-long blonde curly hair

black body

gray head

Fazian Black Knight Parrot

blue eyes

EXPLORER'S VEST

utilities

looks like Dad

Wide wing span

full name: Amerigo Vespucci

modified metal talons for military use

open position

Dad's jacket

EXPLORER'S LEGGINGS

Yak- fiber leggings

tall brown cowhide boots

closed position

ZANDER & PUCCI

Twenty-eight

People poured into the streets around the Snake Gate. It was chaos, smoke streaming into the streets, people screaming, the sound of SteamTrucks and flying machine engines filling my ears.

"What's happening?" an old lady screamed. "What's happening?" No one answered her.

There was another explosion. Smoke rose from a different section of the city and I looked up at the nearly cloudless blue sky, wondering when the next one was going to hit.

I heard the rumbling of more trucks and ducked into

an alley to watch a convoy of olive green SteamTrucks came down from the direction of the base.

But they weren't filled with soldiers. These trucks were filled with trainees. I recognized some of my classmates from the Academy and I called out to a girl named Lily Hart, "Hey, Lily, where's Zander? Is he on the trucks?"

"Yes," Lily called back. "He's back there."

I ran toward the back of the convoy, shouting "Where's Zander? Where's Zander?" Classmates from the Academy tried to point me in the right direction, but they were attempting to organize their gear and stay on the trucks as they rumbled along the uneven roads. Everyone looked terrified.

Finally, I found him, on the last truck, sitting up front with Joyce and Lazlo Nackley. Lazlo was in full military uniform, standing at the back and shouting orders.

The truck convoy had to stop because there were so many people in the streets and when Zander saw me he waved and jumped off the truck.

"What are you doing here?" he said. "You need to get away. They know you escaped."

"Zander," I said. "These people are in danger. The whole city is. We need to get them out of the city."

Zander was about to say something when Lazlo Nackley jumped down and got right in my face, screaming at me.

"There's nowhere to take them," he said. "They need to go back into their houses."

"If they go back into their houses, they will die," I told him. "They're sitting ducks out here. They need to be evacuated."

"We don't have enough trucks to evacuate the city," Zander said. "I tried to convince them, but they said we need them in the desert."

Lazlo started shouting through a bullhorn at all the people in the streets, "Everyone go back to your homes. I repeat. Please go back inside. You are safer indoors than on the street. "

He was right about that at least. We couldn't evacuate them on foot. They'd be even more at risk walking out of the city, a huge target on the road.

What could we do? There wasn't anywhere safe for them. Except…

The tunnels.

Suddenly I remembered the entrance at the Leopard's Gate. If, in fact, I'd found it, it was probably sitting there open right now, just waiting for someone to discover it. I was supposed to protect the secrecy of the locations on the maps at all costs. Who knew who might walk by and get curious?

But the people…

There was another whining scream and then a dull explosion somewhere to the south. It was getting closer. I thought I could hear voices calling out in distress from a few streets over.

"I know a place they can hide," I told Zander and Lazlo Nackley. "I know where they can be safe. You can lead them there."

"This is ridiculous," Lazlo said. "We are in the middle of a military operation."

"We're under attack," someone shouted.

"Where?" Zander asked. "Where should we go?"

"There are tunnels. Underground tunnels," I told him. "They go into the desert. The entrance is behind a shop just down there. You can evacuate them into the tunnels. But you'll need to guide them. It's dark and there could be a stampede if they're not careful. You'll need everyone to help." I described the spot to him.

"We can do it," Zander said, appealing to Lazlo. "I know we can. It won't delay us by more than an hour or two. If we don't do it, these people will die."

"Absolutely not!"

"Lazlo, I'll help. We can do it," Joyce said, standing up.

"We'll help too," someone else said.

Soon, all the trainees were jumping out of the trucks and Lazlo was yelling, "Get back in here. I'll tell my father. You'll be court martialed!" but nobody was listening.

"Thank you," I told Zander.

"We'll get them into the tunnels," He said. "I'll see you when this is all over."

I gave him a long hug.

And then I ran.

I reached the Leopard's Gate in five minutes, running against the tide of people being led toward the tunnels.

Please. Please. Please.

I stood beneath the huge archway and looked up at the place where a wooden drawbridge had once sealed off the city during an attack.

I looked to the right. And then to the left.

And there it was, one block on the inside wall of the archway that was slightly indented and hadn't been indented before. You wouldn't see it unless you were looking for it. I pushed on it. The mechanism behind it felt resistant and sticky, as though it hadn't been activated in years, but finally the wall started to slide inwards, taking the stones below and above it along and opening a door in the wall.

Overhead, I heard the roar of an engine and then another explosion.

I forced myself to look down into the dark space that had opened before me.

I was standing at the top of a long staircase.

Twenty-nine

As soon as I stepped onto the first stair, the blocks slid shut behind me and I switched on my vest light and started down the stairs. The walls all along the staircase were carved with shapes and hieroglyphics. They reminded me of the hieroglyphics I'd seen in Haa'ftep Canyon. But I didn't have time to stop and examine them because now I was at the bottom of the stairs, and as I shone my vest light around, I could see that I'd been right; I'd found the twin city to Simer City, the city that the ancient Simerians had escaped to when things were too dangerous above.

I was now looking at a smaller version of the Lion's Gate and as I stepped through it, my vestlight found a smaller replica of the city above, with its winding streets and sandstone buildings.

It must have taken decades to build, each street and structure lovingly constructed by hand. I imagined the men and women and children who had made it, carefully carrying stones below the city streets. Had the invading army been on its way? But then how would they have had time to make this?

Confused now, I looked around me. This hadn't been built under threat. People fleeing an invading army would have retreated to caves like the ones I'd seen my first day in Simer City.

So why was there a replica down here and why was it only accessible to those who knew the secret of the Leopard Gate?

Most importantly, why had Dad wanted me to come down here?

My light made shadows on the walls and buildings, creating strange shapes that reminded me of continents on a map.

Continents.

In Drowned Man's Canyon and again in King Triton's Lair, Dad had used one map to lead me to another. So where was it?

I started at the Leopard Gate and walked methodically around the perimeter of the underground city. Aboveground, it had taken me five minutes to run from one gate to the other. Down here, it took less than one. In another minute, I was back where I'd started but with no more ideas about why Dad had sent me here than I'd had before. I shined my vestlight around at the walls, searching for the maps that I'd seen in the other places to which he'd led me.

I'd been so sure, when I'd looked up at the stars and realized about the gates being flipped.

The stars.

I took my vest off and held it up so that the light shown on the ceiling.

I'd found the Lost City of Maps.

The ceiling was covered with painted maps of the great cities of the ancient world, mosaics showing the streets and temples of Athens and Babylon and Petra and Simeria.

I imagined someone like me, hiding in the underground city, only needing to look up when he was homesick for the world above.

I thought of the children who must have learned about the world above from these maps—learned about its people, its great works of art, its music and its languages.

But why had Dad wanted me to come here? These were all places I knew about already. These were all places everyone knew about already.

Where was the next map?

I looked around. It had to be hidden somewhere in the underground city. Where could it be?

There had to be a reason Dad had sent me here.

And then it hit me.

The Leopard Gate. The Lion Gate. If the underground city was an exact replica of the city above, then maybe the next map was hidden in the same way the city had been.

I raced to the Lion Gate and sure enough, there was a small leopard embedded in the wall. I pushed on it and it depressed. Then I raced back to the Leopard Gate and found the little lion, just like the one in the wall above ground. I pushed on it too and it depressed, but no stairway opened up, no hidden room revealed itself.

Then I remembered.

Up above, the entrance had been at the Leopard Gate.

Down here, it would be at the Lion Gate. I raced back to the other side of the city and when I pressed on the little leopard this time, it sunk out of sight, revealing a little pocket in the stone.

Inside was a piece of paper.

My heart racing, I removed it.

It was a folded piece of thick parchment, exactly the size and shape of Dad's map of Drowned Man's Canyon.

I was about to open it when suddenly the entire underground city filled with light and I spun around as a voice came to me from somewhere in the labyrinth of streets.

"Amazing, isn't it? I don't think very many people have ever seen that map."

I started, whirling around to find that I wasn't alone.

I felt fear snake through my body.

Standing against the far wall and holding a huge, ornate sword, was Mr. Mountmorris.

Thirty

"Well, open it up," he said, gesturing to the paper I held in my hands. "You must want to see what your father left for you this time."

His eyes were full of excitement. Now that it was light, I could see every inch of the sword he carried and the edge of the blade glittered dangerously.

I looked around, trying to formulate a plan. I was pretty sure I could outrun Mr. Mountmorris, but in order to get out of the underground city, I needed to get back to the Leopard Gate. Stalling for time, I said, "Where is that light coming from? It feels almost like real sunlight."

"Ah, it is real sunlight!" Mr. Mountmorris said. "Do you see those mirrors up around the top of the ceiling? They are reflecting the sunlight from small openings up above and lighting the city. It's very advanced technology. Quite remarkable. Now, aren't you going to open the map?"

"Maybe later," I said, moving quickly to tuck the map inside my vest. I darted towards him, then pivoted and started running back behind the Lion Gate and around the other side of the city. If I could lose him in the maze of streets, I could get back to the Leopard Gate and be aboveground with the map before he knew I was gone.

I took a right turn down a little street, running as quickly as I could. I thought I could hear his feet behind me and I picked up my pace, pretending to turn left then doubling back and taking a right turn on to the replica of the street leading to the central temple. In a few minutes, I had crossed the city and I was heading for the Leopard Gate. But just as I approached it, a tall figure with a spiky red mohawk stepped into my path. Like Mr. Mountmorris, he was holding a sword out in front of him.

"Hello, Mr. West," said Jec Banton.

I heard footsteps behind us and then Mr. Mountmorris was there. They'd caught me.

Mr. Mountmorris put the sword back into the sheath he wore on a belt at his waits. "I don't think we have much time," he said. "But I know you'll need to memorize the map. It's too risky to take it with us or copy it down anywhere. You must know that by now. I think I can get you out of the city before the Indorustans arrive, but there's a chance we'll be captured and we can't risk the Indorustans—or anyone else—finding it. You and I are the only two people alive who have seen it.. Unless we're counting your father of course, and as much as I'd like to count him, we just don't know, do we?"

Thirty-one

I stared at him.

"What's wrong? Didn't you hear me, my boy? Chop, chop. Let's get cracking!"

"But you, you work for the government. It's your fault my father is missing. You sent me to the Simerian desert to get the maps so you could invade the Indorustan Empire." I felt light-headed, completely off-center, as though the world had shifted underneath me and everything had settled in a different place.

"Come on, Mr. West, you yourself have been serving

as a double agent all this time, haven't you? Doing my bidding at the count's palace and at the same time doing your own? Well, I have had a similar arrangement, for quite some time."

"But, Mr. Foley?"

"Mr. Foley, as you have no doubt deduced, is a very bad man, as is Mr. Leo Nackley, and we are going to do everything we can to make sure that neither of them, nor the Indorustan Emperor, finds himself in control of the world."

"So..." I was trying to work it all out in my head. "You're a member of the..."

"The Mapmaker's Guild? Yes, of course I am."

"But... Did my Dad know?"

"Of course he did. Marek told you that your father must have been initiated into the Mapmaker's Guild by the High Mapmaker before him, but Marek didn't know who that was, did he?"

"You?" I couldn't believe it.

"Yes, *moi.*" He grinned mischievously. "Isn't it fun?"

"But you've seen all these maps. Don't you know what it was he was trying to tell us? Don't you know the secret?"

"Alas, I tried to reach the places in these maps," he said. "But I am an old man. I believe, however, that your father did reach all the places or very nearly did. If he is still alive, he may hold the secret. But if he's not, only you can figure out what he was trying to tell us."

I had so many more questions, but from far above, we heard a dull boom and then another and Mr. Mountmorris said, "There will be lots of time for answers to your questions. I think we ought to be going now. Once you've memorized that map, of course."

"But we can't let them find this place," I said.

Mr. Mountmorris grinned. "I think I have an answer to that," he said. "Come on."

I stared at the map for a few minutes, memorizing every detail, and then I replaced it in the wall. When I pushed on the leopard, the wall closed, hiding the map once more.

We climbed the stairs and when we came out on to the streets, the first person I saw through the haze of smoke, was Marek.

I stared at him, utterly bewildered, and only became more bewildered when more people came toward me out of the smoke, everyone watching me.

"Mr. Wooley?" My History of Exploration teacher, Cameron Wooley, smiled grimly and nodded.

"Hi Kit," said a familiar voice, and I looked up to find Maggie—the Academy's headmaster, Hilde Magnusdottir—looking at me too.

"Are they all in the Mapmaker's Guild too?" I asked Mr. Mountmorris.

"Not exactly," he whispered. "Everyone here is a member of a secret resistance organization that is trying to overthrow both the governments of the United States and the Indorustan Empire. We believe in peace and we believe in openness, and we hope that those principles can prevail over the forces of war and control. There is, shall we say, some *overlap* with the Mapmaker's Guild, but no, these friends of ours out here do not know everything. They know only that your survival and your ability to find out what your father was trying to tell you is absolutely critical to our mission and, perhaps, to the survival of our world."

"I'm sorry, Mr. Mountmorris," Jec Banton said, stepping forward. "But I think it's time for you to go."

"Yes," Mr. Mountmorris said. He nodded towards the Leopard Gate and Jec Banton swung the hatchet at the lioness carving, shearing her off completely.

"Ah, here we are," Mr. Mountmorris said and I looked up to find the *Grygia* waiting for us a couple streets over.

"Let's go," Mr. Mountmorris announced and Mr. Wooley and Maggie and Marek stepped forward to join us. Marek shook my hand and patted my back.

"I'm glad you're safe," he said. "There's someone else who wants to say goodbye."

I looked up to find Kemal standing there, his face covered with soot.

"Kemal?" I said. And suddenly I knew. "You were a double agent all along too?"

"I guess you could say that," he said. "In the end, I just wanted to make sure you made it here."

I hugged him. "Thank you, Kemal."

"You're welcome. Be careful."

"You too."

As we headed toward the *Grygia*, we could see tanks from the base had rolled into the street, their guns pointed toward the sky.

"We've chased them off for a little bit," a man in uniform told Mr. Mountmorris. "Should be long enough for you to get out."

Five minutes later we were rising above the city.

"Now," Mr. Mountmorris told me. "I know you have more questions, but let's make sure we're on the right course first."

Maggie and Mr. Wooley were up in the cockpit, talking to the pilot. Marek sat next to me.

"The map you saw in the city," he whispered to me. "What did it show?"

"It showed the far north," I told him. "It looked like a location near the North Pole, but none I've seen on any map."

"All right then," he said. "You give the direction."

"North," I said. "Tell him we want to head north."

"Mr. Banton, please tell the pilot we're headed North," Mr. Mountmorris said before turning to me and grinning.

"Now, let me tell you everything!"

THE END

Acknowledgments

The Expeditioners have had many companions on their journeys. I'm grateful to Esmond Harmsworth and to everyone at McSweeney's who were responsible for sending me on the original adventure.

For making it possible, big thanks go out to Sue and Dave Taylor and Matt, Judson, Abe, and Cora Dunne. I am grateful to Vicki Kuskowski for her beautiful design work, and of course to Katherine Roy for her amazing cover art and illustrations.

Most of all, I want to say thank you to all of the adventuresome readers who told me they wanted more expeditions, and to the librarians, teachers, and booksellers who put books in kids' hands every day. These stories exist because of all of you!

About the Author

S. S. Taylor writes tales of adventure and mystery for kids and grown-ups. She is the author of *The Expeditioners* series, as well as the graphic novel *Amelia Earhart: This Broad Ocean*. You can find out more about her and her work at SSTaylorBooks.com.

About the Illustrator

Katherine Roy is the award-winning author and illustrator of *Neighborhood Sharks* and *How to Be an Elephant*. She is also the illustrator of *Otis and Will Discover the Deep* by Barb Rosenstock and *The Expeditioners* Series by S. S. Taylor. To learn more about her work and research go to katherineroy.com or follow her on Twitter at @KRoyStudio.

CPSIA information can be obtained
at www.ICGtesting.com
Printed in the USA
LVHW032337250919
632328LV00001B/196/P

9 780960 083527